I0534567

CROSS PATHS

A WRIGHT SERIES

Book 6

LINDA MCKOWN

CROSS PATHS

ISBN-13: 978-0-9997357-5-6

Author:
LindaMcKownAuthor LLC
11574 E Running Deer Trail
Scottsdale, AZ 85262
http://www.lindamckown.com

Any names of people and entities are fictitious in this story having been created by the author's imagination.

Front Cover Photo of the book is copyright through Shutterstock. Book title manipulation was done by Joseph McKown

Thank you, my fan readers. See the back page for a list of my other books. I'm glad you are into suspense and hope you enjoy the finale in this series called Cross Paths.

Contents

1   Virginia Woods Surprise

DEREK WAITED ON the gravel road for the police to arrive. The change in temperature was affecting his movements. The weather was cold in Virginia compared to Los Angeles. His raincoat wasn't quite warm enough.

The estate was outside Williamsburg on the York River. The owner recently redid the road into the estate. There were tall trees surrounding the property which showed their leaves turning gold and red. The house looked like a veritable white fortress with huge pillars out front. He wondered how old the house was. The structure's age was hard to tell. His other investigator, Brandon Keller, was with him, because Rhonda Peters took another assignment for Derek. She would be off that assignment in about two days.

The police arrived and blocked the road.

"Hi, I'm Derek Wright and my partner, Brandon Keller, are here courtesy of the Los Angeles police. We have interest in the owner of the estate. There is a woman who currently goes by the name of Kendra Brooks living in the estate. We believe that is not her real name, but then, we don't know her real name. We call her Snake woman, and she is wanted around the world for numerous crimes. She is sought out by us for questioning regarding a murder in Fontana and Los Angeles, California. The Miami police also would like to talk with her about a murder at a salon."

The police detective extended his hands to Derek.

"I'm Harry Jenkins, the one in charge of the case in Virginia. We do have our search warrant but are not sure the owner is home. There is a man and woman who are caretakers staying at the house. They occasionally go boating. We have notified the inland waterway patrol and coast guard in case we need their help tracking down their high-speed boat. We don't know the names of those two people. Here comes the rest of my team. Let's start the process."

"Great, we're ready to get this over and done," said Brandon. He shivered, turning up the collar on his jacket. Brandon put on his leather gloves.

Two police cars accompanied Derek's vehicle and they parked in the large parking area a hundred feet from the house. Approaching the door, Harry knocked on the large double wooden doors and then used the brass knocker and hit the doorbell. They couldn't hear any commotion inside and no one answered. Harry motioned his man to unlock the door with his special tools. Harry, two of his policemen, Derek and Brandon went inside the home.

The house contained a minimum of furniture on the first floor. The kitchen was almost empty of food. Derek wondered if anyone even lived here. Harry and his men went upstairs. Derek and Brandon walked down a long hallway toward the back of the house to what looked like a library. The doorbell triggered a clock within the home, unknown to the visitors. The something was a timebomb.

Pushing one of the library's double panel doors aside, Brandon stepped inside as did Derek with the other door. They heard the tick-tock sound. Then the clock stopped. Derek and Brandon stopped. The hesitation of the clock might be a problem. Two gunshots rang out. Derek and Brandon staggered backward.

Derek saw Brandon was still standing. The man was bent over. Derek scrambled behind the sofa inching closer to Brandon. He didn't see any wires. Next, they heard two shots upstairs. There was no one in the library, just two guns set up to fire when a wire was tripped. Derek saw the wire. There could be more and much more. They were all in danger.

Derek was reminded of Minnow Surf's marijuana farm that blew in Nevada. He yelled, "Back out, the whole house is rigged. *Back out now*."

They heard the men running down the stairs and they all ran toward their vehicles. Derek and Brandon reached the back of their vehicle first and then the other policemen were helping Harry, who appeared to be shot also.

Derek swore, "Man, that hurts."

Harry choked out his words, "Tell me about it."

Brandon was hit in his gun hand and looked white. The hands were always sensitive. Derek opened the back-vehicle hatch and told the two men to sit down. Derek decided that he needed to do was sit as well. Ambulances were summoned and fire trucks.

Ten minutes went by and they could hear the sirens in the distance coming to help them. Derek knew he couldn't call his wife, Jess. She would be on the first plane out and he couldn't have her anywhere near the premises. He called Rhonda to get on the next plane from Los Angeles. He hung up and the ambulance was at the end of the road when the first bomb went off. The sound appeared to be in the location at the back of the house near the library.

A helicopter flew close to the house and made sure the men were outside a minute before the blast.

Five minutes passed, and the ambulance took Harry and Brandon to the hospital. A second ambulance turned the corner when two more bombs went off, levelling the old estate. Derek was taken to the hospital.

The firemen waited for three hours and let everything burn before they approached the structure. They wanted to be sure the bombs were done. The bomb squad arrived to sift through the mess as soon as the water spray cooled things down. The area wouldn't cool down until the next day because there was a basement to the structure. The basement was full of the upper floor debris. A bucket truck and grader were called in to level an opening. A fireman saw a steel door at the left side of the house.

Around midnight, Rhonda approached Derek's room at the hotel. She politely did her signature knock so that he would know who was there.

Derek opened the door to let her in. He changed his bloody shirt for another one, but his bandage was already leaking a little. Rhonda helped him remove the shirt. She went into his bathroom and brought out a large towel and wrapped around him. She went over to the bar and opened the small refrigerator with the hotel key. After pouring him a glass of whiskey, she opened her water.

"Well, this is a very deep mess you have stepped in. I guess Snake woman was more prepared than we thought. We've not seen her use this setup. I'm thinking her two employees had some influence on her party. I called the fire department and they did pry a basement steel door open. Guess what they found in the dark?"

Derek shook his head. The burn marks around his wound were stinging. He didn't have a clue. The pills were finally working, and he put more salve under the bandage area. The hospital didn't want to discharge him until he assured them that he would go to the emergency room to get his bandage changed in the morning. They didn't like his tough guy attitude. Rhonda, as one of his co-workers, was worse than his wife. She informed him that he should been smart and stayed at the hospital. She wasn't cutting him a break.

"There was a new cement tunnel that went under the entrance road and exited out by the culvert."

Derek remembered the location of the culvert. That was the reason for the new road, an escape route. The woman could buy anything she pleased. Her money and contacts made it difficult to catch her.

"I called the police station and the powerboat disappeared. The police watching the boat left their station when the house blew the second and third time. That is when they took off. The coast guard is looking for the boat and any occupants as we speak."

Derek told her that he wanted to see the tunnel in the morning after checking in with the emergency room. Next, they would visit with Brandon and Harry. Rhonda agreed and went directly to her hotel room. She called her husband, Skid, to let him know she arrived. She couldn't tell him about the investigation other than the players were marginally and stubbornly fine. Skid received the message.

Derek called Jess and calmed her down. He asked her to take their yacht out as soon as she could with their daughters. He would call the Cortez brothers for extra security for their son who was visiting in Miami. Jess was familiar with the security drill.

XXXXXX

The next morning, they would find a second tunnel which was something built around the civil war days to hide slaves and favored troops. The second tunnel exited into a hill which housed a newer structure. This building contained a movable roof allowing a helicopter the ability to lift off.

Derek and Rhonda figured Snake woman made her escape that way. The bombs were timed giving her the minutes she required for escape through the narrow tunnel. She rode a special, newly-designed bike that had no spokes, but lighted wheels which would help her see in the dimness of the tunnel. The bike was extremely lightweight and easy to steer. The rubber on the tires was like a dirt bike for traction on the hard-packed earth.

"She may have made her way through the tunnel in five to six minutes, especially if she did practice runs with the bike. I believe she rode this path daily for exercise, because she needed to make sure the helicopter was safe. Once she was at her destination, the timers kicked in. The doorbell set off the clock and we met the guns. She must have walked the theatrical set like we did to make sure of exactly where you boys might be standing."

"How did she know we would ring the doorbell?"

Rhonda looked at Derek.

"Call it woman's intuition. The ensuing gunfire and our confusion were her cover to exit the grounds permanently. The tall trees camouflaged the blades on the helicopter as she flew close to the tree line beyond the hill. She probably flew under those high wires. That shows expert skills, because I know that I wouldn't even attempt the move. She plays dangerously close to death. We have those words in her profile, if you recall."

"Yes, I do remember. You must give her credit; the plan was a perfect escape. Besides skill, she is very brazen and amazingly talented. I wouldn't fly my helicopter under those wires either. She flew directly over us, knowing we put our guns down. We believe she survived a plane crash into the ocean some time ago, so she's like a cat with nine, dare-devil lives. Her ability to find escape in difficult situations is phenomenal."

Rhonda said, "Because the helicopter flew close to the house, she was able to set off the first bomb via a remote device. I'll bet the rest were set to a timer sequence. Snake woman made sure you were out before she blew her house. Chaos major. The question is why?"

Derek wouldn't be so stupid next time. He rubbed his lower left side where the bullet hit. The spot was very sore, much like his temper.

He didn't want to be reminded of Snake woman's perfect plan. He didn't think she was a cat.

"No, she didn't belong to those beautiful creatures. The woman was a thing, a robot, or freak of nature."

He remembered the waves in the Atlantic when he and his wife, Jess, chased after sunken treasure. A calm sea could churn into a nightmare of waves. Snake woman was the wind causing the storm surge.

"A large wave always crests and falls. She is currently on the upside. We will catch her coming down."

Rhonda nodded. She worried the woman would make it to shore on some other newly-designed device. High tech was entering this game of cat and mouse.

"I find her use of guns interesting before making the great escape. Snake woman sent another warning? I like your wave idea. Let's hope she doesn't hurl a volcano at us. Then we'll be facing a tsunami."

Rhonda found the second steel door behind a bookcase in the burned house which held canned goods. Rhonda identified the location of the hidden release when she started moving the smoky glass jars with paralyzed macaroni in them. She didn't like macaroni much, hence the name.

Rhonda didn't know anyone who put macaroni and spaghetti noodles in glass jars especially since they came in a nice box. There were no jars of canned spaghetti sauce, just large cans of tomato sauce.

Snake woman didn't appear to be a woman who enjoyed cooking in the past. Tomato sauce was bland without spices. It was odd which made her more curious. Rhonda would find the garden behind the house with vegetables and massive mounds of herbs. The woman obviously took some classes and knew how to cook or hired excellent chefs. She would add this information to her profile.

She lifted the rest of the cans of artichokes and capers to another shelf. Rhonda found the electronic door opener under a large empty can. The bottom was missing but the label was intact. The closure button was in the same spot on the other side, again covered by a fake can.

"Clever design. Cheap, but functional."

There were oxygen masks and tanks if needed to traverse this tunnel of three hundred yards. They could see where she worked to enhance the structure with new pretreated timbers to keep the older structure from collapse. There were additional metal attachments and an occasional heavy girder at each end. They found new vents in the large yard disguised with a top layer of grass. The vents were impossible to see from the house or the air. An entire new sprinkler system was in place to keep things watered and hidden.

"Nice rabbit hole," commented Rhonda.

They both knew the helicopter would not be found. The item was already in parts and probably was up for auction on the black market.

Derek contemplated and told Rhonda, "The black market is where we will find her."

Rhonda looked alarmed. "There are too many of those types of places. The odds of finding her game in the underground are a million to one."

Derek laughed. "That's quite a number, but you have to remember that Jess will enter the game. She will secretly pursue this woman behind my back. She won't be afraid of a tsunami. Therefore, I need you and the other girls to become my ally. Whatever my wife is up to, you will need to figure out a way to join her."

"You want me to act as an infiltrator to protect and defend your wife?"

"Yes. This game is the worst we've ever encountered. Jess could get hurt. I know she flies *too close to the wire*."

Derek clicked the remote for the building retractable roof and clicked the thing again to reclose it, shutting out the sky. He could imagine the snake woman's face as she lifted off to freedom, leaving the police behind. The police and Derek's team were gnats to her. The woman didn't need to look backwards at the ruin. She had done this same act before.

"Whatever it takes, I want Jess to be safe. She goes way beyond in her eagerness to catch the criminals. I've been protecting her my whole life. This time, I do need help."

"I get that. I'll talk with Tami and Tiare to see what type of force we can bring to the table."

Derek disgustedly threw the remote on the table and took off his gloves.

"I also want Snake woman. The cost will be high, I'm afraid."

Rhonda saw Derek's deadly calm expression. She knew a storm was coming. The sun was setting into a brilliant fire from the low setting clouds. She worried about what was headed their way. A frown crossed her face. Skip would worry about her getting that close to the Snake woman, her evil tricks, and heavily-controlled spheres of influence.

Privately, she said, "Think, girl, where is our badass culprit hiding?"

2   Continuation of Investigation

RHONDA KNEW WOMEN. She thought Snake woman was no different. She must have weaknesses.

"If we find her weaknesses, those faults in her personality might open doors. Maybe we need to run some of this police file information across a personality specialist in the commercial world?"

Weakness number one was a normal concept-- men.

"The reality involved with this woman would end in some rich man's court. Snake woman kept men in her other lives."

The investigation would hang close to the elite folks. There were high stakes involved.

"Maybe volcano was the wrong word, perhaps the word was an earthquake. Could an earthquake help them take her down with a tidal wave? But where does a wave happen. The answer was obvious, the ocean. No, that answer is too simple."

She would need to talk with Jess. She might have some insight that would be helpful. Rhonda would need to juggle her loyalties to both her friends, Derek and Jess. But for now, she wondered which pricey commodity the woman might be chasing besides a man.   She looked at Derek. He was her friend and vice versa. They had been in similar scenarios. This one was heavy.

"Where are you playing my rich bitch? I see who you really are. Do I have the descriptors correct? The descriptors of your personality are the following. Let me park them in a one-page list: emotionless, cruel, utmost cunning, insane beyond a reasonable doubt, death-destroyer personified, and all around off-the-basic of human charts?"

Derek took note of Rhonda's words for their suspect. The words fit. He turned to Rhonda.

"Insanely crazy, rich bitch who murders. I missed off-the-charts."

"Yes, siree."

She touched Derek's arm. Rhonda knew that her boss missed nothing. She was glad to see him return from a dark place. He needed to be fully engaged to work this case. It would be immensely difficult to catch this woman.

"What's her second weakness?"

Rhonda went through the list of murders. Snake woman or Margaret met Matin Domingo in Miami after her husband died. Domingo was a known drug and arms trafficker who was recently caught and placed in jail in Miami. His mistake was hooking up with Minnow Surf. Domingo was poisoned with mamba juice while doing his sentence. Rhonda looked at the snake ring picture and shook her head.

Then there was Boyd Reeker, aka Tiger Sphinx which was a name the police called him. The man was from Africa and terrorized Queenie by hiring the kill of one of her guards at a Miami spa and others. He crossed the line and tried to murder Queenie who is now known to them as, Ara Jones. Ara and Jack Jones helped to catch the evil man. Tiger Sphinx also died from the same poison because the police let slip that the Sphinx was part of the underground world. The police deposited knowledge that Sphinx was possibly a snitch who turned in a long list of criminal names to them.

Ara was the one who gave the police the list with Snake woman's place of business. Snake woman killed the Sphinx for revenge. Her Shannen's Island had to be left behind before the police came. This was her special and favorite hideaway in the Caribbean. Her name while on the island was Shannen Drake. According to police records, Shannen Drake was dead and died in Bermuda. A man who lived with Shannen on the island was Max Lewis except there was little information on him. He was believed to be traveling with her.

"Well, no loss to the world of those two other bad boys. They deserved to be gone from this earth."

Rhonda continued reviewing a person named Theresa Tracker and her boyfriend, Henri Clan. The police believed the two were part of Snake woman's organization and murdered copycat poisoners in Miami.

Next were the murders of Maureen Burrows and her brother, Ed, in Big Bear Lake, California. The brother was Matin Domingo's former lawyer. The Burrows were involved. The death of Sawyer, a retired race car boss was linked to them. The police knew the Burrows couple chased Trent Rudy who was

Sawyer's former race car driver. Both men died, one via murder and the other an accidental drowning.

Finally, there was Rich Madden, the politician who murdered his wife in Los Angeles, California. Later he was murdered by Snake woman's employee, Theresa Tracker.

Again, no loss of any of those people whose own habits fell short on the scale of justice. They were into robbery, theft, extortion, and murder.

Theresa Tracker and Henri Clan were found drowned in a lake in Russia with a small portion of poison in their system. The actual death by drowning was strange. Their snowmobiles drove through a soft spot in the ice, except the machines were tied together. The police weren't sure if the ice cracked and they were trying to help each other except the autopsy showed a small amount of poison in the blood.

"More revenge for what? Yes, their deaths were a colder revenge. No actual blood relationship with Snake woman if she was adopted, yet somehow Theresa was trusted for a while to do Margaret's murder business."

Rhonda picked up the snake ring picture. The ring bothered her that somewhere on the Los Angeles street she saw the same ring on Mr. Clan. Was there a connection to Matin Domingo?"

Rhonda was tapping her ink pen on the table. The ring was some key and was a high-quality design.

"Current day fashionistas would love this design. It was too bad the ring was stolen when Matin died. How could a ring be a weakness?"

Derek could see that Rhonda was circling like he did previously.

"We need to throw out all of our old techniques and ways of catching her. They don't apply anymore. She has changed. She's moved into the twenty-fifth century. Are you ready to explore new technology to rein her in? It will be the only way we catch her. Even if I saw her at some charity event, I would not recognize her. Count on change happening every second with this broad. There's probably been plastic surgery so that she is unrecognizable to us. We need to be super off-chart."

Derek frowned. He hadn't thought of plastic surgery.

"Yes, I'm willing to start totally over. That's what scares me. Her ability to blend in. Twenty-fifth century, huh. Now that's a new angle. Thank you for reminding me that there needs to be exceptional for her case. Let's explore different techniques. Higher technology is required. I've seen the new gadgets at my friend's lab. You remember there was a space company party in Curacao? They can help us. Let me know what you need. I'll, personally buy it and not worry for one second the cost. If what you want is unobtainable, I'm sure there is someone who can deliver. Unknown and undeliverable items are what my space friends have shown me. Only, I believe in my case, they would make an exception on a sale."

Rhonda said, "Skid told me about the Space party in Curacao. I would love to visit their company.

I like undeliverable. That's almost as good as secret and a bazooka."

Derek pointed to the machine arriving in their fly zone.

The police helicopter arrived to take them back to the station, courtesy of Detective Harry Jenkins. They ran to get on board once the blades stopped rotating.

Harry and his captain wanted to capture the evil, torturous woman. She crossed boundaries of countries after she did her rotating, high wire escape act. Harry wanted her behind a different kind of wire. Prison barbed wire was exactly where she belonged, the higher, the better. She almost killed him. Harry would be on the lookout for any clues to capture her. They would start with the missing couple. Then they would find her helicopter.

3   Prior Life

THE SNAKE WOMAN planned the arrangements to have some of the more expensive furniture sold, and the entire Russian complex was sold as well. A new, private account was set up for the transaction of the money deposit. She wiped everything down with bleach at the old house. Her prints and her family's prints must be gone. This location was hard to leave and say goodbye to her parent's former home. She considered them her parents although she knew they adopted her. Her adoptive mother died, and the place was shared with her adoptive father. He became more withdrawn. Then she and her father stopped coming. The furniture was covered, and caretakers watched the place. Eventually, she reopened the Russian complex after her adoptive father became ill. Shortly thereafter, he was gone. This was her second favorite place out of the many she owned.

She lived in Russia for a long time while young. The memories enveloped her. The education of how to do things never stopped. They challenged her to think of better ways at fixing something that was broken. The father would give her three to five items to work and resolve a problem. She excelled in her studies. Her adoptive parents were dead for years now, and she obtained control of their money. Money was not a problem. There would be enough, and there always was opportunity to make more. Opportunity was there in front of her. The object was always bright and shiny.

She drove the truck to their next designated spot. The place was on the map that her friend and lover, Max, left behind. The woman slept inside the old truck and ate a dried beef sandwich. The coffee jug was opened. She felt cramped and a little uncomfortable the next morning. She longed for a warm, hot bath and creature comforts. A good restaurant would have to wait. Orange juice would have been delightful. The juice would have to wait.

Early in the morning, she drove to the small airfield where Max told her to take the truck. She made her transaction with the manager and the transfer of title on the truck to the man. The next day, she called Max to let him know her estimated arrival time. The weather looked clear for flying. She examined the small airplane. The plane looked well-built and maintained. The tires were new. Max did a good job buying the used airplane. She would pilot the plane alone.

That evening, she made her flight calculations and looked at the map with the coast of Ireland. She zeroed into the section close to their small village and the cottage. She examined the height of the cliff lines along the shore. She would need to keep the plane a little higher as she came across the cliffs and into the dry land of farm fields. There was no runway to land near the cottage, except the long road that ran to the north of their property. If she was short, it would be all right as the ditch was lower on the east end. If they needed to tow the plane to the barn, the other truck could handle the task.

She believed the coastline of Ireland was approaching in the distance. The trip had been a long flight. She felt the engine hesitate. Then the engine recovered for a few more miles. The Snake woman told herself the engine hiccup was nothing. The gauge showed gas available. There could have been an air bubble in the gas line. She tapped the gauge. The woman rechecked her distance from the coast. There were only a few more miles to reach dry land. The flight would soon be over.

Snake woman closed her eyes briefly. She was tired. Her body rested on the controls and the plane inched closer. She shook herself awake. There was something wrong. She pulled the plane level again, checked her altitude, and coordinates. She was closer to the coast. Looking out the window, there was a layer of white clouds.

"Could that be my coast?"

The cloud cleared, and she saw cliffs. Everything was on schedule. Her plans were working just fine. Then she looked in alarm at her fuel gauge.

"How can my tank be that close to empty? The tank was all right ten minutes ago. All my calculations were correct. I never fail at this. I don't fail at anything."

She quickly scanned the coast for a place to land. The area showed mostly sheer cliffs. The cliffs would kill her.

"Think, think about the maps you saw last evening. There is a place."

Her mind raced to visually pull the map information into her brain. Her recall was excellent. She couldn't let the cliffs win.

"Perhaps a water landing would work, but where?" She was used to flying a float plane. Those skills would help her. She had been flying since a young girl. Trees, wires, cliffs, and water were objects to maneuver around. She wondered if she could at least soar with the plane.

"No, this model is nose heavy. I would need ballast in the backend to level her."

Frantically, she looked up and down the coast. The engine coughed again as a warning. There wasn't much fuel left in the tank before a nose-dive. Snake woman saw the spot of beach and descended toward it. The landing would be short. She would need to cut the power sooner and hope the plane soared some over the waves. She laughed because there wasn't going to be any fuel left to ditch. She would be saving the environment.

The weight of the plane couldn't be that much. The rig was barely loaded. Snake woman looked at the water and timed the incoming waves. If she could drag the wheels in the back of the wave to slow it down, it might work. She would need to keep her wings high so as not to flip. She grabbed her backpack and looped the straps around her arms. The button was pushed, and a water preserver popped out. She looped the neck over her other arm. She slowed the plane and slid the door partially open and jammed a blanket to hold the door, so she could get out.

The wind swirled around her and sucked her breath away. The airplane controls required and occupied the rest of her thoughts. The plane slowly lowered. The wheels were barely touching the top back of the wave. Her control over the airplane was impressive, if anyone was watching. The drag was enough to slow her speed. She coasted on the wave and then the belly raced across. The plane sunk further into the water. She was ready and slid out the door.

Snake woman felt the cold rush of northern ocean water as she slipped out the door. A wave slammed her around the back of the cab. She grabbed the window edge as the plane floated on what was left of inside air and the wings. She wondered if she had time.

Escaping the plane that was slowly submerging, she thought about her fuel line and made herself look at its location. She could swim toward shore with the life vest or check out something. She dove under the water and examined the underbelly. She attempted to hit the unlock. Finally, the panel opened. She came back up for air and dove back down. Under the water, she felt the fuel line. The cut was bubbling. There was a small hole in the gas line. The cut was smooth and man-made. She realized what happened. Rapidly, she swam upward. The cold water chilled her thoughts.

"Max, how dare you arrange this ending?" She was furious as she popped back to the surface and fresh air. The woman grabbed the floating vest and backpack from the door.

The numbing cold was getting to her hands. She stroked fast and hard to get through the breakers before they pulled her back out again. It was a fight swimming to shore until she got past the entrance to a small cove. Dragging herself onto the beach, she sat and watched the waves drag the plane down the coast breaking its wings on the bottom. She shivered. The sun broke through a cloud and felt good on her skin. She emptied and rung out the water from her clothes.

Looking at the high cliffs, she saw a path that might take her to the top. Someone had built a small handrail on the upper top. The wood looked bleached and worn. The fence may not be secure, but it was better than no rail. There was some placement of stones in spots on the path. She guessed today was her lucky day. The beach was used by people in the past.

4 Tavern and Denny

SNAKE WOMAN WALKED in the early evening light.

"Well, so much for seeing the sights in Ireland."

She scuffed at the dirt. She knew approximately her position on land and was grateful when a road appeared. She read the name of the sign, McCleary Road. The arrow pointed toward smoke in the distance. Walking toward the wood smoke, she entered a small tavern.

The man next to her pounded on the bar. "Come on, Jimmy, I'm hungry."

The man had ordered the corned beef sandwich and beer. The sandwich was filled with a half inch slice of white onion from the garden out back. The tavern seemed to have not heard of salad greens, but cabbage was available. There was a pile of the smelly stuff on the plate. He tasted the cabbage and was surprised by the vinegar and oil and chopped olives. The man whined.

"Oh, for heaven's sake."

The bartender took the plate back, scraped the cabbage into the garbage, and gave the man a portion of raw cabbage.

The bartender said, "Don't ya know, the vinegar and oil belong in the cabbage. The olives add salty taste from Italy. Most of you blokes in here

24

won't touch my mum's wonderful dish. You're missing a lot. Those three items are what keeps me healthy."

The man shrugged and kept eating his order. The bartender looked at the strange woman and told her the turtle mulligan stew was on the menu today and tomorrow.

The man next to her pointed to the chalkboard. "Don't order his wonderful cabbage dish. Make him give it to you plain." He bent around her to get the salt and pepper.

She paid the man no mind because she didn't want to create a scene. Looking where he pointed, she almost gasped. A stuffed pig with real fur and glass eyes held the chalkboard. The pig wore a nametag around its neck. She wondered if the sign was a joke. Evidently, the pig was named Lucky Denny. He didn't look so lucky anymore. His fur was oily where the patrons evidently patted and touched the body.

The woman sighed and whispered, "The pig needs a bath and the other one. Well, he's just another dead bloke. How does a person run into two of them?"

The bartender came over and took her order. The woman didn't seem to talk right and mumbled. He thought she was a bit daft. He figured out that she also wanted the corned beef sandwich with onion. He brought her the wonderful cabbage on the side. He knew that she would like the dish. The bartender brought her beer, deposited her money in the till, and moved to his next customer. The strange visitor kept staring at Lucky which was normal for new people in his bar.

Snake woman's shoes began to dry. Before she reached the tavern, she stopped to take out some of her money so that it would dry. She calculated the amount that she might need to pay her bill. When the bartender complained about the damp bills, she mumbled the beer got spilled, and there were no napkins.

The bartender gave her a rag to wipe the counter and a disposable coaster. There weren't any napkins. They were still in the wash and wouldn't be dry until the supper crowd. He threw her a bag of peanuts.

The Snake woman would be long gone before the turtle soup started cooking tomorrow. She could see the heavy slab of bacon when the swinging doors opened into the kitchen. Turtle anything wasn't what was attracting her attention. Warmth from the tavern fireplace and nutrition from the food was essential.

She asked the bartender if she could buy a small slab of bacon and some bread for her journey south. The bartender wrapped two packages for her. He told her there were a few green squashes in the garden if she liked the stuff. She thanked the man and left, stuffing the green and yellow vegetables in her pack. She would turn north.

The man next to her left. No one else paid her any mind. She was a woman who wore an old coat and hat, stolen from a local farmer. They thought she was a farmer's wife from the next county. She also stole the farmer's hunting knife from the holster on the back porch inside wall and would be using the blade shortly. Snake woman stashed her bag of poison and put a slower-acting syringe in her pocket.

She walked the last five miles before taking her flint and starting a fire. The bacon was on one long stick and the vegetables were on the other. She took her light rain gear out and put them on. She needed to wait a little while in the cold. She thought of the stuffed pig and wondered how it died. The darn thing looked like he wore a smile on its face. Snake woman thought she was losing it.

"Forget the pig. They probably turned him into liverwurst with a jellied crust."

Chewing on the crusty dark bread, she looked at the loaf.

"The bread is marbled."

She held the loaf closer to the fire.

"Oh, good grief. The bread is green and brown pumpernickel with dry oatmeal on the top. He told me the loaf was his specialty. He must have baked the bread for the mulligan stew fest and parade. That means everyone will be at the tavern tomorrow. That's good news. The taste isn't too bad, rather goes with the whole countryside. See what you're missing Denny."

She sniffed the air. Her bacon was burning. She took the vegetables off sooner. Supper would be vegetables and a few pieces of inner sides of the bacon.

Snake woman believed her friend would be up awaiting news of the small airplane that crashed. The fact that there was no body wouldn't worry Max. The ocean could have taken a floating object a distance down shore. She hoped the plane was still drifting for a long way and would be miles from where she landed.

"Actually, I hope the riptide carries the lot out to deeper depths."

The lost plane would give her time to complete her last mission with Max.

"Pieces and parts would be good."

She kicked the coals brighter and checked the time on her waterproof watch. She left the burned bacon in the grass for the night critters.

"I need time."

5   Prior Residence - Ireland

SNAKE WOMAN WAS always good at taking care of herself and waiting. At two o'clock in the morning, she found her and Max's residence in Ireland. The place was exactly where she remembered. The wooden shed at the edge of the property was her first clue after the decrepit sign on the road that read, Meander House. The road into the cottage wound like a drunken cow coming into the barnyard for milking. They had laughed about the road. The road would be difficult to traverse in the winter. They were going to make changes to the road. Now there would be nothing done to the place because no one would be living there for very long.

In the distance, she saw the barn. There would be plenty of time later to enter the house and hold her daughter. Hiding in the small barn in the hay mow on her property in Ireland, she slept soundly. The lost airplane in the depths of the ocean no longer mattered. She was alive.

Suddenly, she jerked awake. Her dream of swimming in the cold water brought her awake. She was cold. The engine sound drew her attention and made her sit up. Max started the truck to warm the engine. She peered through a knot-hole in the wood and saw Max leave in the truck. The time was ten o'clock in the morning. She saw the horse and the motorbike in the barn. Max must have filled the horse's bins with food and water while she slept. This was dangerous for her to be so close. Her plans began to formulate. She would give the horse enough food and water for two days and take the motorbike. Snake woman would have liked to steal the truck but decided it would be too noticeable. The fact that Max took the truck was good. She palmed her new identification card. This would be easy.

The nanny arrived and opened the cottage door. Max must have met her on the road. The nanny went inside. Snake woman would have to wait. She was all right with the waiting. She would have time to explore the surrounding area. At noon, the nanny went outside to hang up some clothes. Snake woman slipped inside and stole a can of soup, crackers, and cheese from the refrigerator. In the evening, the nanny left. She remembered what Max told her about the babysitting arrangements.

On a whim, she followed the nanny. What would one more day cost her. She figured, absolutely nothing. Max had not yet returned. The child must be asleep. The older woman was less than five feet tall and seemed to be overweight. It was hard to tell from her heavy wool garments. They were approaching an older white-washed house set on a hill. The house looked like someone added four additions onto the structure, making the house seem disproportionately ugly against the stark landscape. There were amazingly beautiful bare trees and bushes that dotted the trail to the nanny's house. There was no smoke coming from the chimney. The possibility occurred to her that no one else inhabited the space.

Snake woman noticed the small garden. One of the additions looked strange like there was a greenhouse of some sort. The windows were grimy, but she thought she saw some small trees inside when a small piece of lighting hit. A few raindrops fell. The nanny was a gardener of sorts. She wondered what she grew in there?

"Do I think the woman is growing weed or pot? No, she doesn't look the type to smoke."

Snake woman hid behind a large grove of trees. The rain drops were getting larger. The nanny turned back as if she heard something. Her grey scarf slipped from her mouse-brown hair. Snake woman fingered her syringe. The nanny was the ugliest woman that she had ever seen. She reminded her of an alligator she saw once north of Orlando, Florida.

"What are you doing, Max Lewis, with this woman? Normally, your tastes edge toward beautiful. Guess this was the closest person available for the job of taking care of our daughter."

The anger she felt toward Max removed all their years together. There would be swiftness. Nothing would stop the flow of evil thoughts in Snake woman's brain. Revenge ruled her every thought for now. She turned and went back to Max's cottage.

She opened the small refrigerator door and was glad Max was still gone. She saw the tube of liverwurst from the butcher shop. The label read one pound and there was a quarter of the nasty stuff left.

Snake woman pulled out the syringe and inserted the needle into the meat. Murder was the appropriate thing for her to do.

Next, she checked on her daughter. The baby was sleeping. She touched her child.

"Still, the nanny shouldn't have left her all alone."

She knew that it was time to return to her hidden spot and wait some more. She watched from the other crack in the siding to make sure Max returned. She would recheck things in the morning and give the poison time to work. Snake woman couldn't let his mistake pass. She would have to get herself a new man someday or keep her desires under control if she was going to truly raise her daughter.

The next morning, she heard whistling and looked out to see Max getting water from the old well. She heard the nanny approach. Her crunching old boots on the partial gravel driveway were a dead giveaway. The poison didn't work. Max Lewis was still alive. The nanny and Max were in conversation.

"Max hadn't eaten the liverwurst."

Snake woman would need to wait and rethink a new plan. She left the old barn and found her bag of poison stash and grabbed a heavy, fast dose syringe and fondled the knife. She stopped and put a second syringe in her pocket just for her protection. Killing Max had turned into a harder task to accomplish than she thought. There wasn't much time. He would become suspicious if her body wasn't found soon. The sea usually gave up its dead.

The time was noon and the nanny left Max's cottage.

"Why is she leaving my baby so soon? Max must be coming shortly." She waited a half hour. There was no Max. Snake woman snuck into the cottage and opened the refrigerator.

"The liverwurst was gone."

She checked the garbage can and saw there was no paper wrapper. It dawned on her what possibly happened. She needed to follow the nanny once more. Her legs ran across fields, taking shortcuts off the road. As she was approaching, she saw the old woman. The nanny skipped and danced a little bit outside her cottage. Snake woman couldn't believe what she saw next. Then the nanny bent down, holding out a bite of liverwurst from the refrigerator package to two white geese.

"Oh, no!" said Snake woman. She came out from her hiding place startling the nanny who almost dropped a piece on the ground.

"Don't feed the geese that meat or they will surely get ill. They should only eat grains."

The nanny turned and grinned.

"Who are you? Are you lost and from the next county? Or are you a beggar wanting this meat? Well, you can't have any. I've got myself and friends to feed."

Then she popped the small bit of liverwurst in her mouth and swallowed. Suddenly, she teeter-tottered and fell.

33

Snake woman grabbed the meat package. She didn't want the geese to eat any. She let the nanny fall backward into the soft pond mud. The geese went flying and squawking as far away from the two women that they could get. They knew when to run.

Snake woman approached and saw that the nanny wasn't dead. No one was around. She could drag the nanny's body into the pond. The body would drift to the other side, pushed by the wind. This was a small town, and their local doctor would take a little while to figure out how the nanny died. Max should be at their home right now, so she couldn't steal her child. Snake woman only needed a little more time. This required a change in her plans.

Taking a branch, she scraped the muddy area to remove her footprints. She took the package of liverwurst over to some large boulders and buried it. She saw a decrepit wooden wheelbarrow next to the greenhouse and retrieved the object. Placing the nanny's limp body into the bucket, she headed towards the house hoping the doors were not locked. The raindrops hit her face and suddenly there was a torrent of water as she reached the door. The wind whipped the door from her hands, and she sat the body in a wooden chair before she could shut the heavy door.

There was an old phone near the chair. She lifted the receiver and was thankful that the line was dead. Checking the old woman's pockets, there wasn't any cell phone, only an opened package of cigarettes.

"I didn't think you were into the modern age of communication. All a person has to do is look at this relic of a house."

Snake woman called out while walking through the house. As she suspected, there was no one else at home. She started a fire with the wood stacked in the fireplace. A vase with dried lilies caught her attention. On a whim, she threw them in the fire. A brief memory hit her brain.

Next, she dragged the heavy woman's body into a bedroom with old lace curtains and a faded flower bedspread. A nightie hung on the door hook. She put the nightie on the nanny and took her wet and muddy clothes into the laundry room. She was surprised to see an electric washer, but no dryer. She dumped the clothes inside and added soap. The washer clicked as the machine worked its cycles.

"At least the power isn't out to this house. Therefore, what is with the phone?" There were other things to worry about.

In the meantime, she checked out all the upper rooms. The view of the green rolling hills was exceptional. The location of the house was a realtor's dream. She found an ancient trunk with pictures inside. They were old and crinkled. A photograph and envelope address caught her eye. A canceled check was in the papers for the Title to the house. Another document was a trust fund for the occupant's living expenses and payment of taxes for twenty-five years.

She read the inscription and gasped. "Oh, no!" Snake woman read the letter. She wondered how this old woman could have been that attractive in her younger days. The black and white photo showed youth and vitality. Snake woman pocketed the photo, letter, Title, and trust document. She would need to research the funds remaining through her lawyer. This place was legally and technically her property. The land was worth more than the house.

Snake woman slammed the lid down on the trunk. Her anger flared. She would have to deal with this second issue later. For now, there was the greenhouse to inspect.

The greenhouse showed a brick wall separating the glass structure from the house. She assumed the builder thought about the separation as a firewall. The greenhouse contained pots and pots of starter lilies under a grow light. The lilies surprised her, and the smell brought up a memory again. She dismissed the brief thought.

Small seedling plants in a corner box looked suspiciously like marijuana. She smelled a leaf.

"Oh, yeah, smoking lift for the nanny's day."

In the other corner was an old wooden refrigerator. The key was sitting on top of the empty box. She wondered why the refrigerator was in the greenhouse. On a whim, she locked the door closed. She slipped the key in her pocket.

Next, she went into a library and found a glass box with very old pistols inside with four shells. She took out one of the pistols and placed two shells inside. Stepping through the back door again, she aimed at the large tree and fired two shots. She hit exactly where she wanted. The small branch snapped off and flew away. The tree was left with two marks. The marks were hers. Snake woman smiled. She formulated her new, very slippery plan in her mind.

"There would be a need to keep witnesses to a minimum."

She went back into the house, found some cleaning supplies, and put the cleaned pistol back in the glass box. The blast hadn't awakened the nanny. Taking out the photo again, she went to the fireplace.

Slowly, Snake woman dropped the photo in the flames. She watched as her father's signature curled, and his love message turned into ash and smoke. This old woman once was her own nanny and her adopted father's lover. Her adopted father owned the house and twenty-five acres.

"How odd to have found you this way, old woman. I've been looking for you for a long time. I wonder if Max knows who you are? Of course, he doesn't know. I only briefly mentioned you with much disdain."

"This meeting must be fate. Now everything makes sense in those last years of my adoptive parent's lives. The bickering was the crumbling of their marriage. Who killed my mother? I don't have to assume any more. You were responsible for her death. My father was devastated at the loss of my mother, but he let you go. First, he banished you from our lives rather than tell the police. The letter explains everything. Do you remember me? I doubt it as your eyes look foggy from possible vision problems. We'll have to see, won't we?"

She acknowledged to herself that she should have left the old woman to die near the pond. Now a decision would have to be made. However, the timing was wrong. The nanny's presence was still required.

"There's time to walk and time to dance in the future."

Snake woman went back into the bedroom.

The nanny finally awakened. There was an old metal ashtray on the nightstand with a half-burnt, hand-rolled cigarette butt. The old woman tried to reach for it. Snake woman pushed the ashtray out of reach.

"I guess looks can be deceiving. I thought you lost your breath when you tripped and fell by the pond. You need to wait a little while because smoking right now will get you into trouble."

"No, it won't. Where are my pack of cigarettes?"

The woman hadn't been out too long, only three hours. Snake woman congratulated herself for not killing her yet. She didn't like the woman one bit and the feelings appeared to be mutual. The woman lived alone for too long and was almost antisocial, plus cranky.

"I don't know where you placed your smokes. Can't you remember?"

"No, I feel fuzzy."

"The fuzziness is probably from the large stick when you fell on it. You could have poked your eyes out." Her explanation to the nanny would contain lies. The nanny frowned and felt her head. Her eyes were still there. The stranger made her feel awkward and unsafe. Fear showed in her eyes briefly.

Snake woman watched her closely for recognition and didn't see any enlightenment. As a stranger in the house, she scanned the room again. There was nothing, but dullness as the sun set. Turning on the antique bedside lamp, she went to the kitchen and brought back crackers and tea. The old woman ate and drank a little bit of both.

"You must have developed a touch of the flu and fell over. Or perhaps it's your age causing some problems." Snake woman went on to further add that it was a good thing that she came along to help a neighbor.

"We could say that today is almost your lucky day."

"Why is my day almost lucky? I smell beer. Have you been down to the local pub? Or did you drink my stash?"

Snake woman saw confusion in her eyes except the old woman's brain was sharp, like a tack. That could be a problem.

"I never saw you as a neighbor before today."

Snake woman sighed. Perhaps she should have eaten more of the liverwurst. It was too bad she buried the morsel. "My name is Laura Reafer and I'm Max's sister." She almost said Lewis as the last name. Max changed his id to Reafer and she did the same.

The nanny frowned. She didn't believe this Laura person. Max didn't mention a sister or any woman for that matter. The man she worked for didn't talk very much. The nanny knew he hadn't told her about Laura. Suspicion arose in the old woman's breast. She didn't like this stranger called Laura.

"I'll be taking care of the baby at the cottage from now on. Max has left to get married and he will be gone on his honeymoon."

The nanny still looked doubtful when Laura told her that her services were no longer needed.

The old woman tried to rise. "But I need the money."

Snake woman could see the nanny counted on receiving that money. She exited the room, found her backpack, and Laura peeled off two hundred dollars. She came back into the stale-smelling room and handed the woman the bills. She told her that the bills were severance pay that Max asked her to give the babysitter.

The nanny felt better and then her eyes closed again, and she fell sound asleep.

"Finally, we are done talking."

The next morning, Snake woman stepped into the library to make a call. She waited, because she found the loose wires on the wall telephone and reconnected the device temporarily. The telephone started to ring. She slowly picked up the receiver. Max began talking. She wondered why Max called. Fabricating her voice to the nanny's speech and tone, she let him know that she could watch the child. It was all right for him to leave. She would be there within the hour once she pulled her food supplies.

Laura, the Snake woman, went into the house's pantry and filled a sack with supplies. She spotted the peach jars and put three in the bag. The old woman was still out snoring. She wrapped the old woman's leg in gauze and some wood splints. Laura figured the trick would slow the legs down. She found some homemade beer in the refrigerator, opened the bottle and smelled. Drinking half the bottle, she next placed the beer close to the ashtray with a small piece of cheese. The scene was set. If not, the room set would at least create more confusion in the old woman's brain.

Quickly Snake woman moved toward Max's cottage dressed in the old woman's clothes she selected from the closet. She put on the old scarf and waved to Max as he was driving away from his cottage. She couldn't believe her good luck. He believed she was the nanny.

6   The Irish Constable

TWO WEEKS LATER, the local constable arrived at Max's cottage. Laura let him into the cottage and finished feeding her child some squash she found in the garden and pureed.

"Your neighbor said that you have killed the owner of this house, Max Reafer, with one of her pistols from her library, and placed him in her greenhouse refrigerator freezer. She says you stole the key. She's also missing some items from her closet and her pantry, specifically peach jam. The woman wants her jars of jam back. The jars are real special were her words. The woman was in a panic. She thinks that you may be did push her near the pond and caused her leg problems."

Laura looked innocently at the constable and inwardly wasn't surprised at all. The nanny had no clue who she was messing with.

"Did you know the nanny told me she does hallucinate on occasion. Is it possible her mind has wandered a bit? I'm not anywhere near her size in clothes, and I'm the one that helped her into the house after she fell. I did see strong homemade beer in her refrigerator. Maybe that's also part of the problem. I have heard from Max and he is just fine, happy as a lark, to quote him. He has a new bride. Oh, and Max does have several jars of jam in his pantry. Perhaps she forgot when she gave them to him as a gift. One of the jars has been opened, but you can pick up the other two. I'm not fond of peaches."

The constable looked flustered. He didn't want to come out in this thunderstorm to harass anyone. He mistakenly stopped at Ms. Barnes' house to make sure her electricity was working when the crazy old woman told him this horrific story.

"If you could come to the nanny's house, then we can put this mix-up to bed."

"Sure, no problem," said Snake woman as she fingered the refrigerator key next to a syringe that she always carried.

Sure enough, the key was laying in an empty pot near the wooden refrigerator in the greenhouse, and the constable opened the door. There was nothing inside the refrigerator except a small empty container. Snake woman commented that she didn't know the house contained a library. She wondered if she could borrow some books to read sometime in the future.

The constable put the two peach jars on the kitchen counter of the old woman's home. He walked Laura back to Max's cottage, apologized, and left.

"Oh, if Max does call, have him ring my number so we are certain that he is fine."

"Absolutely, I will give him your message." The baby awakened, and Laura told the constable goodnight.

In the early morning, Snake woman went back to the greenhouse and planted her device. She put the marijuana plants in the refrigerator container. Laura knew exactly where Max was located. She sent him on a wild goose chase to search for the woman from the downed airplane who seemed to have amnesia and was wandering the countryside.

She picked up her disposable phone and made the last call to Max. She disguised her voice as a young Asian woman the first time she called him. That's when he called the cottage and made permanent babysitting arrangements with the nanny. Only, it was Laura who had the job, unknown to Max.

On the second call on the burner phone, she told Max that her Asian step-father would deliver the message of where the downed pilot was staying. She gave Max the directions for the meeting because the address wasn't locatable via coordinates on any guidance systems. Only the stepfather knew the place; she didn't. There was an old castle location that crumbled down over the years. A few bricks and mortar remained. Only the destitute hung out there now, but usually were gone by noon. The stepfather would meet him there. Max had no idea what he would run into.

Snake woman put on her makeup, wig, and clothes. She found a silk kimono in the nanny's trunk that she stole. Resewing the item into a jacket and using some hair from an old doll, her disguise was complete. She put the note in a plastic bag sealed shut. She poured coffee into the newly purchased mug and wrapped the venison burgers in wax paper. She put a green toothpick in the sandwich that contained the peach jam. The peach jam smelled strange. Laura didn't eat the jam. She believed something was wrong with the stuff. Laura hopped on the motorbike and left her daughter sleeping.

"This was a necessary move. So far things were moving smoothly. My little one will be asleep until I return."

Before she left, Snake woman went into the small room and tenderly touched her daughter. She was a pretty child and continued in her sleep state.

"We will only be a little longer. I'm glad that you are a quiet child who takes naps. This will work. We will be a great escape team. There will be lots of adventure for us in our future together. The time has come to say goodbye to Max. His life, unfortunately, will end. His lack of loyalty and stealing you away are the reasons for his downfall. A person always needs to be prepared."

Two weeks later, the constable reappeared at Max's cottage. Laura opened the door to let him in for coffee.

"No coffee for me this time. We have a slight problem."

Laura looked at him.

"Is the old woman mad again in her mind?"

The constable scratched his beard. "No, we found a dead body up north twenty-five miles, and there was a truck nearby that matches Max Reafer's vehicle. We believe the body may be Mr. Reafer due to the tall size. No one around here comes close in height. Can you come with me to identify the body?"

"All right, but I must bring my child, and someone will have to watch her for me."

The constable watched Laura and he didn't see any tears. Perhaps she didn't believe the victim was Reafer's body.

"How did the body die, if I might ask?"

"We believe he slipped or fell off the cliff and maybe drowned," said the constable.

"Oh, that must have been horrible. An accident, surely."

"Don't know. There wasn't much in the truck nor a cell phone either."

When they arrived at the morgue, the coroner was out ill. The only person was the nurse who took Laura into the room for the viewing. The nurse handed the plastic bag to Laura after she identified the body as her brother.

Snake woman knew how to act. She walked slowly as if stunned, holding the note outward in her hand to the constable. He took the bag and read the note.

"Well, it seems to have been a suicide as his girlfriend bowed out of their upcoming marriage. Poor guy."

Laura looked sad and let a tear slip. "Did anyone find a gold ring or maybe he gave the jewelry back to the girlfriend?"

The nurse handed her the small bag containing Max's things. No ring was found.

"I'm perfectly fine. Maybe the girlfriend needed the ring, or he hocked it for money for their honeymoon. I'm sorry that I never got his girlfriend's complete name. You don't think the wedding was a scam to get money out of my brother, do you? Wouldn't that be terrible?"

The constable only shook his head.

"Maybe they can find some DNA somewhere or any substance. Usually, men don't fall off a cliff. There's always a possibility something turned the man besides a friend. Although the impact must have taken his breath away."

"Indeed, the cliffs here are steep."

The constable rubbed his stubby chin. "The nurse is good and can find most anything. I'll have to check on Ms. Barnes. She's probably heard the news about her past employer."

XXXXX

In a month, Snake woman's lawyer sold the house, furniture, bike, truck, and horse. She was moving. She drove over to the nanny's place in her recently checked out rental car.

No one answered the door, bell, or knocker. She could see a figure in the greenhouse. The geese were by the pond. A few packages were by the door, awaiting the mailman to pick up. She went back to her car and moved the vehicle down the road, hidden by large bushes. The mail truck arrived at the nanny's house and drove off with two packages. The top package was addressed to the constable.

Snake woman waited to make sure the mail truck was down the road. After twenty minutes, she moved closer to the house. She heard the nanny singing. Snake woman hit the remote device and walked to her car. As snake woman drove away, she said, "Final vengeance, nanny, from my adoptive mother." Watching the glow in the rearview mirror was of short duration. Her thoughts were racing forward.

Her new airplane was waiting at a private airfield, fueled and ready-to-go. The passports and new identification papers were in her bag. She undid the zipper on the side pocket of her teal knit dress and felt the gold snake ring. Her dress showed decorative zippers which concealed a poison syringe as well. She smiled. She and her daughter were flying to Africa.

There was a small run-down house she purchased there for a song. She would store the plane in some building a couple miles away. Africa was where there existed plenty of gold. Snake woman decided to enter the gold trade. Her teal-colored heels tapped on the floor to the music on the radio. She would find a place in London or Paris and a school for her daughter.

She suddenly realized what the nanny put in the two packages for the mailman. Everyone in the area tasted the nanny's jam last year. However, the jam's shelf life expired. The nanny's jam contained a form of botulism in those last jars. The nanny always bragged about a special ingredient. The town's folks believed the ingredient was malt.

The botulism caused Max pain as he tried to reach for the Asian woman. There was no need to use a poison syringe. Too late did knowledge dawn on him who the woman was at the cliff's edge. Snake woman's speed in getting out of the way as he tried to lunge toward her sent him spiraling over the cliff. He was out before he hit the ocean.

Max's body was cremated, and his ashes were thrown off the same cliff. She thought briefly of Max who finally recognized her after he ate half the venison sandwich.

"Your burial was the least that I could do. I reneged on brutal. You were one of the luckier ones or not. It's all a matter of perspective."

Snake woman checked the weather forecast and the day was perfect for flying with her daughter. There was no one that would interfere in her life. Enemies wouldn't find her or her family. Two of them were dead.

7   Arrival in Mali, Africa

SNAKE WOMAN EXITED the commercial airline, found a rental car, and drove to her plant. The plant was currently one of her safety zones. She had many. She walked the aisles. Everything seemed to be fine with the products and workers. There was no hurry, just a rapid pace. Today was Friday and pay day. Snake woman wondered about Monday. Would the workers still perform?

She picked up a special marked box and went into a private room with her foreman. She checked the contents in the white jar with a copper-colored cap. Taking off the cap, she lifted the plastic lid and smelled the exquisite beauty crème. Using a coffee spoon, she dug out the cream and threw it in the garbage can. She lifted the last piece of plastic insert and saw the gold. It was worth the tortuous wait. The jar was part of a special shipment.

Snake woman handed her foreman the almost empty jar. The gold was his month's payment as an employee. That was the way they transacted their fraudulent business. His name didn't show anywhere in the business accounts. The locals knew where the man worked. He quickly pocketed the gold in his handkerchief.

Replacing the lid, he put the empty jar back into the carton and taped it shut with heavy translucent tape. The flaps would be taped a second time with brown tape to match the rest of the shipment. He put his initials on the side of the box for the receiving end to take the carton from its pallet. The special box would be delivered to the same woman at her warehouse in London.

"Yes, this is ready for shipment to England, Ms. Ashley. I am pleased with the contents."

"You remembered to counter the weight with a few empty jars. That is good. Thank you, Akash."

She turned to leave. "Oh, please send one jar with only the cream to my daughter at her school in London. She really likes the stuff."

The man bowed and nodded. Akash wouldn't mail the jar but would give it to the human resource person who kept all the confidential papers. She would mail the package. He was only trusted with the gold.

Akash knew not to cross the woman in front of him. He saw her gold ring and believed the ring was a bad omen. A snake was a vile thing to him. Snakes were like a wise man with no arms that poisoned people. The woman's eyes didn't blink very much either, like a serpent. She was not an enchantress, but an actress on an evil scale.

Akash and his partner applied for positions at her company. His partner disappeared after the first interview. The partner was never found. Akash was upset and came to talk with his employer. She told him, "Sometimes the winner takes all. It is too bad your partner chose the wrong side. Congratulations, you have won the job."

Akash told her that he didn't want to win this way.

"The choice wasn't his to make. He entered willingly into the game. He is gone."

She didn't tell Akash that she turned the man over to the police for stealing her supplies and selling them on the streets. She knew fear would work in her favor to control the man.

Akash was afraid of her and her game. Right this minute he was thinking Kenya was a better place to live. He thought possibly somewhere in the Lamu district working on a sesame seed farm would work. The region was perfect to grow sesame or a simsim crop twice a year. He was strong and could work long hours. Akash liked both types of seeds, the whitish or the black natural seed. The Lamu area was along the coast. The problem was money. Money was required to travel and live on the coast. Working for Ms. Ashley would give him cash, albeit via an illegal route. He did illegal many times before except this time the imprisonment would be higher if caught.

Snake woman watched her victim's discomfort and indecision. Then he nodded.

He would fit in just fine in her organization.

"A little fear is a good thing in business, no?"

She smiled at her new employee. He bowed and left her.

Snake woman drove to her boyfriend's place of business. He was a gold investor, one of many in Mali, but he was the richest. That was why she picked him. He also was single and wanted to stay that way.

The man wasn't half bad at anything. He would do for the time being.

The man was fascinated by this woman. He ran into her accidentally on his business highway. She had flown into one of the mine's airstrips as an investor in her own private plane. The woman wore white khaki's and shirt with snakeskin heels to a goldmine location which was filled with heavy equipment and dust. She stood out like gold particles on a sluice conveyor belt. He was impressed. Bryce Hatcher thought of her as a valuable business associate and potential playmate. He welcomed her into his life. She was glad. They fit each other perfectly.

Opening the door to his office, she would have to wait, because he became detained. She fingered his name plate on his desk, Bryce Hatcher. He was born in Australia but lived in London previously. She lived sometimes at his flat in Mali but would now have to use it temporarily until she could find another hideaway.

"There you are. How did the sale of your house go in America?"

"Hello, Hatch. The sale already was completed last month. I just vacated the lease a week sooner than planned. Your helicopter is also sold. I have wired the money into your account."

He came over and gave her a kiss. "Good, I'm glad that old place is gone. I wasn't into Georgian furniture or a formidable palace."

Snake woman frowned, because he really had no clue who she truly was or that she barely escaped the police in Williamsburg, Virginia. Her instincts told her to rig the small guns and explosives before she left, just in case. She was glad that she did. The devastation would slow the police down and remove evidence. The new owner could always rebuild on their insurance policy. She read about the three police who were slightly injured.

Hatch saw that she was disappearing someplace in her world. He thought she was thinking about her business. Now was the moment to share with her some of his feelings. All women wanted to be compensated for their time. Hatch was large in the compensation department. Besides, there were other tom-cats looking at his woman. He couldn't have that happen. Moving to his locked desk drawer, he opened a drawer and handed her a small black velvet box. He didn't see her frown.

A jewelry box worried her in this unsafe town. There were many thieves. Mostly, they either worked for him or her. Plus, she wasn't sure what commitment this piece would cost her. She was surprised and needed to react appropriately. Snake woman hadn't expected the present and told him so. She opened the box and lifted the heavy necklace out.

"You bought my favorite design, the *serpentine* in gold."

She was pleased that he remembered their last conversation of liking the curving, winding design.

There was a large ten carat emerald cut diamond dangling from the chain.

"And you remembered my favorite color stone."

Hatch was pleased when she came over to kiss him more properly. She forgot to say that he also bought her favorite stones. She was toying with him a little today. He liked it when she was on her toes. Fun was on the horizon. Both worked hard, and it would soon be time for play. He knew her visit would be an enjoyable one.

"You do know that I care for you and your child very much, Danielle."

This was the first time he mentioned her child. She didn't want to talk to him about her personal affairs. He fastened the necklace which had a twenty-inch chain. The diamond landed where he wanted to see it.

She touched the gem and laughed for the first time in several days. Things were moving smoothly with her new boyfriend and partner. He was ahead of her plans. She remembered the sputter of her small plane flying into the Irish coast.

The gem was worth her efforts. She was the one who bought his helicopter under a fictitious company name. The helicopter was in a shop being repainted and reupholstered. The engine would be checked and cleaned up. The helicopter was a good backup plan if she couldn't reach her plane. Danielle decided not to tell him. There was no need. The man was bright but not as smart as Max had been. There were times she wished Max was still alive. Then, she caught herself. Sentimentalism was never her style. Love sometimes is a boomerang.

"I checked my shipment and the boxed load looks fine," said Danielle.

"You did not hire any children for this first job, because I won't have any part of child labor."

"No, we are clean. My business arrangements shouldn't concern you."

Now Hatch frowned. She had a way of turning a nice moment into the opposite direction. He didn't want her to bring police into his arena. Police would interfere in his business. He was the spider and his network in Mali gold was extensive. There were people who found gold and bought gold from the weak. He was one of those investors. Hatch once told her. He worried about her comment about her business arrangements.

"My people only employ the best. The best in this business are over sixteen years of age. I know these facts, because the young people don't make it very far on two dollars a day if they find some gold in their tiny holes that they have dug. My people work the larger sphere and are in the big game. The holes and mines are larger from which they steal nuggets or bargain a good price for me. I like the fifty thousand-dollar nuggets which accidentally stumble into my domain."

Hatch knew they were both buying gold in the underworld market to profit their companies. He didn't know she smuggled the gold out via her cream.

The office door opened. Hatch's secretary walked into the room. "There's a phone call from Lachlan Thomas for you, sir."

"Hello, Ms. Ashley, how nice to see you have made your way back to Bamako. I'm sorry we are having all this August rain. The wetness does not help the mining operations other than to keep the dust down."

Danielle nodded as the secretary left the office.

"I must take this call. I will see you this evening. The call is from my competitor, Lachlan Thomas. I wonder what his problem is this time."

Hatch put the call on his computer. Lachlan's image appeared.

Danielle knew that she was dismissed. She picked up the empty box and would remove the necklace and conceal it back inside the box before she left the secure building. The necklace was a target for all the poor poachers in the area.

Thinking about the man, Lachlan, she smiled. The last time Danielle was here, they met accidentally at a street side café. Surprised how good looking he was, they talked about their favorite vacation spots. Lachlan told her that he liked diving and went snorkeling with his brother in the Caribbean islands on a large catamaran. The catamaran was so large, a scuba craft fit on the top deck and could be lowered through the center of the craft once the boat was at anchor. His brother was a genius at fixing the catamaran to accommodate his gear. Danielle was fascinated and told him that she would love to see the catamaran sometime in the future. She wondered if there were other catamarans in the vicinity.

The next time that Lachlan saw her at Hatch's mine, he acted surprised. It would not have been good for Hatch to believe the man and woman were already friends. The idea was Danielle's to keep their connection secret.

"Call me Lachlan. Where did you come from Danielle?"

At that meeting, Hatch moved quickly between the two people.

"Sorry, mate, but she's leaving," said Hatch.

Lachlan looked disappointed. "Next time works fine with me." He waved goodbye to Danielle.

She remembered there were some sparks between them. Snake woman would have to be careful. She needed Hatch or Bryce for a little longer. Her daughter was her priority. Real play could wait. She wasn't afraid of the spider man or his gossamer net. Lachlan, however, was interesting and could be valuable in the future.

Snake woman didn't feel fear. She also didn't love, other than her daughter. Plans were made to take care of her daughter if something bad happened to herself. Danielle knew bad luck was just a degree. Her ability to slither away from harm was excellent.

Danielle would use both men to her advantage until she accumulated enough gold to last a hundred lifetimes. More money always helped smooth out the day. Danielle didn't know there were other rumblings happening that would interfere with her plans. She adjusted her snake ring. The object belonged to someone she knew a long time ago. The ring was modified into a smaller size.

She stepped out into the rain.

"At least, the moisture will wash away the stains of the earth, or possibly reveal the true reason for being in this god-forsaken place."

There were way too many people. She preferred remote locations, devoid of the human element. She was already checking places to retire permanently once her daughter graduated from school. She missed her island location. The island didn't lack in creature comforts and only those she chose could visit. Snake woman needed an escape plan past Africa. She would work harder on finding her next safe place. Concentration and focus were her specialty.

"If it weren't for the gold, I wouldn't be here."

She was a distance away from the man leaning against a stone wall. The man watched her leave. She knew that he was a bodyguard hired by Hatch. He hadn't told her about the man. This upset her a little bit, but she knew how to ditch the man when she needed. She was an expert at disappearing as well.

Danielle Ashley drove slowly so as not to lose the bodyguard. She pulled into her five-star hotel parking lot and went inside to the hotel concierge for check-in. A chauffeur would pick her up this evening and take her to Hatch's villa for dinner. She didn't unpack, but took a shower, getting ready for their date. She was glad that there would be no staying at this hotel in the future. Stepping out of the shower, dripping wet, she wrapped a large towel around her body and opened the jewelry box again.

Danielle carefully examined the diamond. It was high quality. She carefully unpacked her black cocktail dress and heels. The sheer fabric reminded her of silk gossamer threads. The packed luggage was set next to the door. She poured herself a glass of bottled water.

"Costume time."

The limousine picked her up. The outside had been newly washed, and a fine layer of dust already was accumulating on the sides. She slid into leather luxury and wealth. The elegant car was what was expected from a mine investor. There would no longer be a nine-year-old girl scared out of her wits. On occasion, her mind slipped into her past. There was a glimmer of a conscious and then the useless thing would be gone. Her superior intelligence threw it out into the barnyard and manure pile.

Danielle was no longer afraid of the dark or anything else. Years of experience taught her the proper way for her to live. She had no regrets about anything. Right and wrong emotions never blipped across her visual screen. The number of dead bodies were part of the things thrown away. She lost count.

The chauffeur closed the limousine door. His uniform was a magnet for the street people who turned their heads to watch. Entertainment was watching the rich. A limousine meant money and big town executives. A person never knew when you would see them again. The executives disappeared into the night much like the precious gold did. It was best to not remember faces, dates, or times or else you were put on a hit list either by the police or the criminals.

The street people were smart in evil ways. Evil ones were to be skirted around. Temptation occasionally flirted across the street people's feeble minds. The feeble were always dead shortly in this gold territory. Bodies weren't found. It was a warning to the other feeble-minded to keep them in their place. Street people confirmed their thoughts with each other. Hushed voices talked about disappearances. Disappearances happened many times a day. They were part of the outcast of society. It was better to be an alive outcast on the streets than not.

8   Nightmare

THE WOMAN GASPED in fright. The scene was the same nightmare. She hoped her arrival in Mali, Africa, would have stopped the dream. She had fallen asleep and dusk was settling in the horizon. Maura Dane crawled out of bed and looked out her hotel window. Down the street, a neon sign clicked on and advertised the bar's wares. The hotel concierge told her the bar was not a good place for a single woman to visit after the evening hours.

Right now, Maura wished she was there having a good time with someone. The evening was early, she would be safe. She missed her dead husband, Guy Dane, and calculated her money would last her for five more years. Her man tried to provide for her every need, but his heart gave out one day at work. He dropped dead and that's when her nightmares started.

She recalled the vision and frowned. The vision was always the same. Maura was in a room and it was raining. Suddenly, an ugly man peered into the room. His vision at the window made her jump every time. She thought she saw a devil. The vision was a man's strange hair, a lopsided smile, and shirt which appeared red. The only thing was the shirt turned white where the rain water hit. She worried that the red was blood. If the shirt contained blood, how did it get there? She didn't want to know. Nor did she want him to come inside the room.

Putting her heels on, she left the desolate room and went down to the hotel bar. Placing herself at the end of the bar which gave a full view of the lobby, she ordered a gin and tonic. There were a few patrons in the bar but nothing noteworthy to peak her interest. The waiter brought her an appetizer menu.

Maura was suddenly hungry for something fried. The menu showed chicken wings with battered okra.

Instead, Maura ordered the wings and a hot sauce to dip them in. The waiter brought her the fried okra as a treat. She bit into the okra and sighed. She was amazed that a chef could ruin batter by putting in slimy okra. The skin on the plant always gave her the willies.

The bartender noted her distress and recommended the appetizer called *dodo*. He explained to her the grilled plantain delicacy and brought her a sample. Maura was not impressed so he brought her fried yams instead. The yams came with a sweet sauce which matched her mood.

The bartender was delighted he finally appeased the lonely hotel guest. She was a chatty person and told him about Southern fried sweet potatoes and sweet potato pie made in America. Maura told him the pie was like a silken pumpkin. The bartender scratched his head. Their hotel chef would never serve pumpkin. Pumpkin was never on their menu. There was only a squash puree used as a slivered decoration in swirls around the main item. No pumpkin was allowed in the hotel. He figured the item of pumpkin must be an American thing.

Eating her last bite, she asked for the check. Her credit card was lain on the counter. Out of the corner of her eye, she saw an exotic looking woman dressed to the nines wearing a beautiful green emerald. The elegant woman stepped into a limousine. The hotel clerk loaded her luggage into the limo.

Obviously, the woman was leaving the hotel. Maura had seen her the day before and wanted to meet with her. Rich women meant rich men followed. Now she missed her chance to get to know the woman.

Maura wanted to ask her about the man that visited her in the lobby conference room. She saw the two enter the room and disappear for an hour. Maura wondered about the man in the conference room. She would later learn that it was a competitor of Mr. Bryce Hatcher's. She caught the man's first name, Lachlan. The exotic woman met a newer, younger, good-looking gold investor.

Maura did her research and found out the other investor's name.

"Lachlan Thomas, what are you up to?"

The conference room contained drapes that could be pulled. There was a beautiful couch with chairs, executive table, media gear plus bathroom, and private bar. Maura knew the couple were having a love tryst. She had not been born yesterday.

Maura asked the friendly bartender if he knew who the beautiful woman was. She was told the woman was Danielle Ashley, a cosmetic facial creme designer from London. The woman was in town checking on her current inventory and was visiting a friend in the gold business, Bryce Hatcher. Mr. Hatcher was well-known in the area. The Hatcher mine was on the tour schedule, and she could possibly catch the mine tour the next morning.

Intrigue was on the venue with the Lachlan person thought Maura. She was sure of it and wanted to scope out the details. Maura was entering the scene as a first-class snoop.

The woman crunched on her last bite of fried food and gooey chicken. The bartender bent over to take her card. She snatched it from his hand and ordered another drink. There was no need to travel to the neon-sign lit bar. Bravery entered the picture with more liquor.

She was going to look up Bryce Hatcher on the internet and get on the bus for a mine tour. She was a brazen woman in her prime of life. If this Bryce man was in the gold business, she wondered if he needed a mistress when the exotic woman was out of town.

Maura was sure that she could fit the bill in that category. She was glad she left her return flight open. This opportunity was something that she wasn't going to waste. Plans were reeling in her head.

Maybe Maura could become a customer and attend any of the exotic woman's publicity events. All the cosmetic designers held events. London was their territory and this woman's territory. The exotic woman traversed London, Paris, and Africa easily.

She could see how easily the woman moved with caravans of limousines. It was difficult to rent a limo in these parts of Africa without assets.

Why did the exotic woman choose that route, the limousine route, when a rental car was way cheaper? Private limos divulged nothing where rental cars did divulge all their routes and clients to the territories and states. Governments monitored rental cars, but not private companies that disappeared in the night. Curiosity hit Maura in the nose.

She needed to satisfy her curiosity. Secrecy meant hidden. Hidden meant money. Blackmail was a select part of money. Moneyed-blackmail was payback. Payback always happened. Luck opened the door. Maura sat on the bar stool feeling blessed. Her husband told her that she was good at catching things. Her skills would benefit her in the future. Maura believed her dead husband. He had been her past ticket. The exotic woman could be her new ticket. All she needed to do was hitch a ride.

The doors just opened for Maura again. Her future looked brighter. She twisted the bar napkin around her finger. Bryce Hatcher and Danielle Ashley's name were written on the tan fabric. The name of the woman's cream, *XM,* was included next to Danielle. *Gold* was written next to Bryce. Lachlan was written in a softer style all alone. She figured already that he was going to be the fall guy in this scenario. Maura wanted the Bryce person. He was her target. She calculated Lachlan would be the loser.

When the bartender wasn't looking, she put the napkin in her purse.

The nightmare vision she experienced earlier was pushed far from the tourist's mind. Maura Dane rode the elevator to the top floor of the hotel and there was no one on the top floor. It was a sign to her that she was safe. The elevator door closed. She then hit the button to her floor, number seven. The number was her lucky number. Seven was the day she married her first husband.

Maura tried to remember what all her lucky numbers were from her other marriages, and she couldn't count. There were seven magistrates. Maura could only remember five. There was a dark period of drugs where the world merged into sand. She loved that period of her life. It was the best. Now she was facing her normal reality.

She walked back to her room smiling. Tomorrow was filled with promises. There was just enough time to order bread, fruit, and special cheese before she went to bed. At the last minute, she canceled her order. This was not a good time to indulge and get fat. Skinny was on the horizon if she wanted a man again. Hippie sweet life was rolling past her brain. What did normal matter? She was going to hitch a ride to her future. She opened the bottled water the maid left and went to bed.

Maura didn't understand both Bryce and Lachlan were out of her league. She would meet someone else from Finland. Thunder was building. Nothing normal was in the forecast. The weather was working against plans. Lightning would roll. Time would fold into itself. The players in the game would emerge and each one would grab at opportunity.

9   Hatcher and Lachlan

HATCHER PLAYED WITH the glass paperweight. The object was a gift from Danielle. She picked the paperweight up at a gift store. Inside was a tiny fleck of real gold. The man he was waiting for was late.

Lachlan entered the room. He had a good idea what the subject would be. Lachlan sat down and folded his arms.

Bryce Hatcher said, "I heard from a friend that you have been talking with strangers. The people in town are from a firm out of Seattle."

"The Seattle people were at my mine and looked at the depth of the next layers. They drilled a sample and will have the ore tested."

Hatcher knew what the outcome of the test would be. The deeper layer on Lachlan's property showed promise. The ore contained gold.

"My offer to purchase your mine still stands. Your equipment is old, and you can't afford to buy new or used."

Lachlan went to the coffee machine and poured the dark brew. Slowly ripping the silver wrapper open, he deposited the cream and stirred. He picked up the sugar packet and put the thing down. He hated fake sweetener. Taking his time sipping the coffee irritated Hatcher.

"Well, what's it going to be? I don't have all day."

"As I recall, you are the one who invited me to your little party."

"And you take advantage by making me wait."

"No, I'm stirring my coffee like I normally do at this time of the morning. Your offer was one-third the value of my mine. I'm not pleased. Consequently, there will be exploration for a more profitable exchange. I also have my condominium in Hong Kong which I could sell. I don't wish to go that route. Is that all we have on your busy schedule to discuss today? If so, I'll leave your offer where it belongs, on the floor, with the rest of the trash."

Lachlan finished his coffee and threw the cup into the trash to further his point.

Hatcher became red in the face. His anger was building. He did have one more item.

"Leave my friend, Danielle Ashley alone. She is my property. A rumor has spread from the hotel staff. I'm protective of what's mine and can cause you grave trouble, if you get my meaning."

Lachlan was surprised the man found out about their meetings or guessed. He knew how to play hard ball.

"I don't take kindly to people threatening me. Besides, Danielle is her own business person and can choose whomever she wishes to associate with. We have been talking about my mine. She has money and expressed an interest as a buyer."

This surprised Hatcher. He hadn't known his girlfriend would interfere with his business transactions.

"I'll talk with her about why she would choose your mine for a deal. I'll explain all the downfalls to her. She's already associated with a big mine. Big in every way. Why would she want a small one?"

"Small? You're wrong about more than the mine. But, you do that. Tell Danielle. I believe she knows gold. Oh, I hear that some gold is missing from your mine. I find it interesting that you have not gone to the authorities. They wouldn't be pleased if a rumor got out."

Hatcher was losing control of the meeting. The man was now threatening him.

"We are looking for any potential errors into our recent losses. This could be an accounting error. I'm sure you understand our logic. Rumors are a problem, too. Police are only a last resort."

Hatcher shuffled some papers on his desk and put the paperweight on them. "You walk a fine line with them more than I do."

Lachlan wasn't sure if his competitor was talking about the police, rumors, or women. He couldn't help but throw in the last dig.

"I'll ask Danielle to meet me at my home in the future. She will be glad to get away from your spies."

The tension in the room between them was explosive. Lachlan turned his back on the enemy and walked out the door. His mine was full of riches. He knew where the best gold pockets were on his property. The new investors wouldn't be told about those gems. Lachlan confidently entered his vehicle with his security man. Danielle insisted he get a bodyguard. Right now, he was glad she suggested the idea.

Mr. Hatcher waited until his known enemy drove off. There would be no contract for him with Lachlan's mine. Disappointment would come later. His anger was not easily extinguished. He threw the paperweight at the metal door. The glass exploded into tiny pieces. His security man came hurriedly into the room to check on the boss.

Hatcher said, "Clean it up and get me a new one."

He worried about how to approach Danielle. It wouldn't work to get her dander raised against him. Once Hatcher made her mad. She stopped seeing him totally. It took many pieces of jewelry and gold to win her back.

"That was a close call."

His security guard thought Mr. Hatcher was talking to him.

"Yes, sir. Right away. I'll get a new one. No one will ever know."

The hidden bug recording device was in the base of the crystal and was deposited in the trash. The new crystal object purchased wouldn't contain the bug.

Hatcher worried and didn't know if there was more to Lachlan and Danielle or not. He wouldn't investigate any further. The issue would come up again and again in his mind, eroding his confidence in their relationship.

There was a missing plug in his organization. Gold was being taken from his mine. The thieves were everywhere. Competition came around every hole and corner in the streets of Mali. Hatcher, himself, smuggled out his gold. There were many places to hide the small rocks. He didn't want to pay the government any of his profits either. Hatcher made the mistake of telling Danielle about his hiding gold from the government. He even told her where he kept the wares.

10 Brita

DANIELLE SAW MAURA watch her whenever she came to the hotel. She wasn't worried about Maura too much. The worry was the hotel employee, Brita, whom she followed to Hatch's office.

Lachlan warned Danielle about someone feeding rumors about them to his competitor. Danielle knew that she needed to plug that hole. Women were always tricky to deal with. Their loyalty could turn against you in a second. Usually, money worked.

The next time Danielle went to the hotel conference room, Lachlan stayed away. She called the front desk of the hotel and asked for some tea and biscuits be delivered. She knew who was going to deliver the order.

The hotel employee entered the room and deposited her tray.

"Brita, do you have a few minutes to talk with me. I have a problem that needs solving."

"Yes, Ms. Ashley, I can talk with you. Is there a problem with the hotel's service?"

"No, the problem is with an employee that isn't paid properly. I see her skills and believe she would enjoy employment elsewhere at triple her current salary. But there could be other employees at this hotel who might be interested, too. My dilemma is how to select the correct one and let them know."

"You don't have to look much further. I'm very good with numbers, taking orders, and cleaning. I can also cook a hearty meal on occasion. I know a little bit about the construction business having taken some college classes. My uncle worked for a construction place in London, too. I know how to fix cars to run or not run."

Danielle heard the last three sentences.

"What about airplane engines?"

Brita brightened, "An engine is an engine. I learn fast. My mind remembers."

"Indeed, those are great skills. I am impressed the more we talk," said Danielle.

"To tell you the truth, I want to get out of this hotel job. I've been secretly watching you. You are admirable, and I would be a good employee."

Brita was selling herself. The interview worked.

"That is wonderful to hear. However, due to the extra money and occasional bonuses, I need someone highly skilled in the listening and reporting categories. Your other abilities may be used later."

Brita puffed up her chest and sat in the chair. She pulled her chair closer to a potential employer.

"I can listen for you. People have secrets and say things. You want me to be your spy. I would love to do the job. Women understand me. Spying can mean danger. I watch spy movies with gas explosions. Those are the best scenes. Because of the danger, there will be bonuses, yes? How big do you think the prizes will be?"

Danielle knew her bait worked. The cheese was the prize. This woman appeared stupid but was exceptionally shrewd. Shrewd was an asset.

"If you can wrap your head around this complicated job, I'm thinking you could retire and live anywhere you want. The money would be your ticket. But first, you would need to apply and earn your wage. The job could be for a long period of time, if you want it."

"Where is my application?"

Danielle handed the completed application to her. The job was at Mr. Hatcher's home as a kitchen maid.

"I need you to complete your personal information and sign the document. Let me take care of the delivery. You will be getting a call soon. The final acceptance paper will say that your employer is Mr. Hatcher. You and I know otherwise. All information regarding Mr. Hatcher will be provided to me weekly. I want to know names of clients, when they arrived, and left. Of course, anything you hear is important."

"How will I know when there's a bonus involved?"

"You let me worry about that minor detail. Many of Mr. Hatcher's meetings could be the trigger."

Brita said, "I understand. You do not need to worry about me. I can do this job."

"Thank you, Brita. Remember no one must know or the job would be terminated. Termination would go on your record and that's not a good thing in Mali."

Brita didn't want to end this new job. She stood up and shook Danielle's hand. Danielle was glad the woman was on her side, otherwise she would have ended their relationship. The hotel would have lost an employee one way or another. Danielle knew Brita was a risk, but she had to take no more chances. Hatch could be a problem in her plans. Danielle didn't trust him. A jilted lover could mean fallout. She rarely trusted anyone, and Hatch just moved to the top of her list.

"I'll let you know how you can send your weekly communication to me. We shouldn't be seen together."

"Yes, that would kill the job and then there would be no golden prize. I want those prizes in my basket."

"The prizes and salary must be deposited in a bank. Here is the bank that you will use. It is one of the more secure ones in town."

Danielle nodded. "Brita, don't tell your sister about us. Good day."

There was now a human bug at Hatch's home. There wasn't any way to plant a new device in the man's office. He hired a company to do a sweep once a week at his plant buildings. Obviously, Hatch was getting paranoid. She hurried to Hatch's office to deposit the application in his in basket. She would make sure he saw the application and read about Brita's skills. Danielle would vouch for her professionalism having seen Brita at the hotel. Brita would find herself newly employed by the Hatcher Mine Company.

11   Five Years Later

TIME SLOWLY PASSED, and the files would be reviewed. Derek was ready for his meeting with Rhonda. She came bustling into the room. Her cheeks were still flushed from her jump out a sky-diver airplane with an old friend.

"How's Randy Moore?"

Rhonda laughed. "He is getting better than I am. I told him that it was because he had more muscles than I do."

"Yes, I remember he always looked to be in excellent shape. Besides the exercise room in his fancy house showed up in his profile facts."

"We were glad that he wasn't the bad guy."

Derek frowned. "He walked the line."

"I know he did. The bikers all do. It's in their nature to stretch things a little, just like we do."

Derek now laughed. "Touché. I should know better. Messing with a woman and her opinion of another man gets me into trouble. Let's open our folders, shall we, and concentrate on a true enigma. Snake woman has been dormant for five years. The length of time is a huge surprise to all of us. We're thinking that maybe we just haven't found the bodies yet. The earth usually gives up its dead if we dig deep enough. Where can she have gone that's deep enough?"

Rhonda looked contemplative. "How about a pit? I'm thinking perhaps mineral."

"Mineral rather than metal."

Derek flipped his personal computer open and typed in a few lines. He sat back in the black leather conference chair.

"Gold is very high right now in the market. The mineral has been doing well for over the last five years. It would be a good choice. We'll keep that thought in the back of our minds for now. We may very well want to readdress those ideas. How many gold companies can there be in the world?"

"Lots, unfortunately, which makes for better cover. She is a master in the art of camouflage. I will, however, begin checking with our contacts on any strange activity with gold companies."

"Good, let's see what else you have come up with that we might use."

Rhonda laid out a few potential scenarios that she ran across.

"Snake woman could have been a foundling child adopted by her second set of parents. It would explain the inability to find birth records prior to this event. Many charities didn't keep good records of abandoned children in their homes. They were too busy trying to feed and take care of them. There were also homes that didn't take good care of them at all. Some children were tortured or barely slaves for the hospital that fed them. Therefore, we don't know her real parents. Maybe the adoption agency didn't either. That's the piece of the missing puzzle. Let's say the second adoptive mother died by accident in one of their homemade labs. Her untimely death could have added to the numbness or lack of empathy for humans that we see in our murder suspect. Her scientist father goes a little more insane from his wife's death and loses his job. That could have added to the duress and the desire to enter illegal activities. The daughter became the father's focus and he teaches her everything, like flying airplanes. There's mostly the bad stuff like the laboratory, and the art of escape.

"I believe the father taught her much. We know from his passport that he traveled extensively to Russia before and after his wife's death. The area is the same vicinity Theresa and her boyfriend were murdered. He also made a few trips to Ireland."

Rhonda continued, "The father dies, and she eventually takes over his business. At the time of his death, her knowledge and skills are comparable to some type of wonder woman. I bet she's even a black belt in karate among other things. She may have climbed Mt. Everest for all we know."

"That is an interesting story, Rhonda, but I do need hard facts, not speculation."

Rhonda slid a second folder over to him. It showed a picture of a child of nine years old in black and white. There was a stamp on the girl's suitcase which read Jamaica and a part of a stamp. The partial stamp was probably Bermuda. The name on her blouse was Margaret. Another photograph showed a man and woman's picture which were photos from a scientific company in England.

"The names of the two scientists were listed. They matched the name of the husband and wife on the adoption papers. A letter was included of the two people's dates of employment. Their specialty was creating anti-serum for poisons."

Next, were copies of their death certificates which showed three years apart.

"The scientist names were Emily and John Ward. There used to be a single nanny with only a last name which shows as Barnes. The nanny disappeared as we can't seem to find someone her age in the system. There is a picture of the nanny smiling and holding white flowers, possibly lilies. After the adoptive parent's deaths, the child, age seventeen, was placed in another home through the services of social workers."

There was one last document.

"This is a copy of the case on the child named Margaret Ward from the police in England. This document closed the file because they believed the child had died in a fire along with the foster parents."

Rhonda handed Derek a newspaper clipping of a seventeen-year-old girl who was found walking around the area with amnesia.

"So, the young woman, Margaret Ward, didn't die in the fire and was possibly the amnesia person?"

"The amnesia person eventually remembered her name and went to live with friends of the Wards. Their names were Rachel and Ronald McLaughlin. Meanwhile, Margaret inherited her parent's laboratory and their home. Rachel was a nurse. Unfortunately for her, she contracted a strange illness and died. Her husband was an older man, another scientist who worked at the same company as the Wards."

Derek saw the marriage certificate.

"Ronald McLaughlin married the amnesia victim, Margaret Ward. There are no pictures, but we have her signature on the wedding certificate. Anyway, we assume that it is hers."

The pattern of latent evil emerged.

"Margaret Ward's husband accidentally fell down the stairs and died of his injuries four years after their marriage. Margaret sold his rich estate and disappeared from England."

"This is excellent research. Did you ask our people to do a projection of what the child might look like today?"

"I did and here is what they came up with. Unfortunately, an aging woman can and does change her looks nowadays with fillers and plastic surgery. I'm thinking the photo might help with her child's description. It's possible Snake woman's real parents were from Jamaica or Bermuda. We have no actual data about her real parents. It might be helpful to talk with some genetics people."

"All right. You can take the time off from our other work to check some of this development out. I think we are onto some good tracing of her past and possible present. I would lay odds the Snake woman's child is in some prestigious school in England or possibly France. This makes sense because the scientific company has locations in both places. It's all we have for now. You might want to find out where the adoptive parents are buried. Snake woman may possibly visit the site."

Rhonda grabbed a water from Derek's cooler, picked up her file copies, and exited the conference room. She was going to contact Tami Cortez to talk with her about the woman's files.

Derek sat in his chair and rubbed his shoulder where an old scar remained from Snake woman's surprise bullet in Virginia.

"Fire and smoke. Mysterious disappearance and deaths at an early age."

Dangerous chills ran through his body. This information rattled him more than the guns. Margaret knew other kill methods which possibly were at her disposal. The poison was only a piece used recently.

The chess board was a controlled game. The players changed or was each chess set different? Derek knew each move she made was well-thought-out in advance. The board was rigged in her favor. We're not even sure if her real name was Margaret. It was a name the orphanage gave her. Derek thought about ID's and passports. Now, she probably purchased them through the underground by the hundreds or thousands.

Derek would continue to call her Snake woman. He would talk to his wife, Jess, about the chessboard concept and mention the gold idea. She would know what to do with the new revelations and the possible woman's past. It was time to go home.

Handing the files to his secretary, Derek mentioned they were private. The secretary knew where to place them in their safe, secure storage room.

12   Jailbreak

HAMM ROE SHOVED the heavy laundry cart toward the awaiting cleaning company's truck. He breathed in the smell of the outside air. The prison was making minestrone soup again because it was Friday. He moved away from the cart to allow the prison guard to check the cart for anybody such as an escaping prisoner. The cart only contained sweaty clothing. The sheets would be on the cleaning roster for tomorrow.

The guard gave the all clear and Hamm pushed the cart inside the truck. Hamm swiped one of the guard's slacks and stuffed the clothing inside his prison jumpsuit. No one was the wiser to Hamm's actions. Next time, he would steal the shirt and tie. He rationalized acquiring shoes would be a problem. He looked at his sneakers and wondered if he could steal another pair and paint them black.

Hamm didn't like this prison guard. The man was meticulous about checking the laundry bin. The other guard barely checked. He hoped next week the other guard would be on duty. This was critical because that's when Hamm would make his move. He needed to get out of this den of prison jocks and their war games.

There were three men from the Green Stream Nevada group in this prison. He overheard their plans for escape which would be during their litter pickup project. The prison took the inmates in a van to clean up the ditches in the highways of Los Angeles. The men were talking about plastic pieces to a gun that they found in the ditch close to a cemetery. The men managed to glue everything together except for the gun handle. They were trying to figure out how to camouflage the hole. Green duct tape was required, and the prison shop only carried the aluminum gray color. The three men kept eyeing the green socks of the prison guards which matched the color of the gun. Plans were made to steal the socks from the laundry. They made Hamm do the theft job in exchange for their group not hurting him. Hamm gladly agreed.

Hamm knew exactly when and the time that the Green Stream Nevada group were going to try their escape. He would coincide his escape a half hour early so the cleaning truck would be past the prison gates. The prison guards wouldn't miss him because there were trainees next week in the laundry detail, and the prison guard wouldn't remember how many men he was supposed to return to their cells.

It would be the first time in a long time that a person managed to escape from this prison. Derek Wright would receive the police incident report and shudder at the knowledge Hamm, the former Stew Avery, a convicted murderer was on the streets again. Their investigative team would wonder if Hamm was running toward Mexico or Montreal, Canada. His cousin had moved to Mexico a month earlier. Derek checked Annabelle's whereabouts, Hamm Roe's wife.

She was Minnow Surf's sister and had married Hamm while he was in prison. Annabelle told her family that she was on vacation in the Caribbean. When they checked her apartment, her car was still there but the motorcycle she bought was missing. Ten thousand dollars in cash was the last withdrawal from her bank account a week before Hamm's escape. Rhonda and Derek believed they were camping in out-of-the-way RV parks and campgrounds in a tent.

Hamm had stolen, what he thought was a real diamond and platinum necklace, from Louisa Renaliere while in Italy. He almost lost his life by Santan Chesin, who found out the necklace was paste in Dakar. An ancient scope from Derek and Jess's home was confiscated by Hamm and his cousin. There was a gold antiquity from Elizabeth Banks' lockbox which he absconded. He drove stolen cars to illegal clients for Minnow Surf's chop-shop operation. Next, he tried to steal gold antiquities and silver coins from a book sale that the Wrights held. That theft is what put him in prison. Before that sale, he killed two brothers, one of which was employed by an auction house.

On the scale of bad people, Hamm was moving toward the top. His good luck at a smooth exit from the prison yards wouldn't continue in his future. Sticky and perilous people would move in. That wouldn't count his pissing off Annabelle. His father didn't even know his son, Stew Avery, aka Hamm Roe was in prison.

Derek wasn't worried about Hamm coming after his family. He knew the bad guy learned his lesson. The Wrights' group of crony families were everywhere. Jess, also, was too dangerous to be around with Derek's heavy artillery. *Or so Derek thought.*

13   Designer Outfit

DEREK PUSHED THE button on his steering wheel of the sports car. The Bluetooth device would connect to make the call to Jess.

"Hi, honey, I'll be a little late. The traffic is very heavy or there's an accident up ahead."

"No problem. I'll eat my salad and you can eat when you arrive on the yacht. Let me tell the chef. I'm in our bedroom finishing the final touches on the designer slacks. The clothing is part of my moon phase project. The puff pom-pom ball items arrived. Now I don't know what to do with them. The outfit looks better without them. The under part is maybe missing. You'll be surprised, I promise."

"Surprise and promises sound good to me. Talk to you when I arrive."

Derek reached their one-hundred-and-sixty-foot yacht called the Silver Zephyr. They hadn't gotten around to building a new home on their property. For the present, they preferred the familiarity and protection of their yacht.

He opened the door to their bedroom and there stood Jess in her outfit. He quickly shut the door. She wore a white slack with a white crop top. The sides of the slacks were decorated with cut out moons in various phases from the top to the bottom with the full moon as the start. The crop top showed the same band of moons going across the front. The fabric was a shiny, delicately sheer fabric. Derek was stunned.

"Too much?"

Derek thought about his words. "For me, no, I love to see you in see-through. Maybe some lining would be good in strategic spots."

"That's exactly what I thought. But the holes are perfect in the fabric. The outfit has to be perfect for the Paris fashion show."

Derek vaguely remembered a conversation about her entry of designs. The competition was heavy this year. Jess wasn't sure she would be allowed into the event as a designer. The fashion designer entry was a big deal to her.

"You forgot about my entry?"

"I hate to admit. It slipped my mind."

Jess's eyes sparkled. And she did a little burlesque dance with the zippers.

"I'm in! They want me."

Derek moved over to his talented wife and touched her bare skin.

"I want you. The moon shapes are right-on. I wouldn't change them. They will look great in Paris."

Jess picked up the designer bag that went with the collection. The bag was white with pale blue lining and the same moons were in the strap design.

"Nice. What about the shoes? Also, you might try to offer the bag in a pale blue color as well."

Jess said, "Excellent. I have your authorization to spend the money on the shoe design? The cost will be expensive."

Derek laughed, "No more than everything else about you. What's a couple more thousands of dollars?"

Jess jumped into his arms and hugged him. His generosity was too much. He started kissing her all over and making his fingers move in circles. He got one zipper halfway down on the pants. Jess pushed him away.

"I forgot to show you the moon phase pom-pom shapes." She held out the box.

Derek picked out three pom-poms and threw them at her one by one.

"Look, honey, a moon fight. You should put a packet in each bag. Or maybe attach comets to the moon pom-poms."

"No, on the comet design. None of my evening gown dresses will have the current fashion of extra back fabric to trip my models on the runway. Who came up with that crazy design? The fabric looks like a stupid tail. Women aren't donkeys."

Derek was enjoying the conversation. He decided to tease his wife and play along.

"Aren't donkeys another word for burrow or jackass?"

"You are shrewd today and full of it. Do you know a jackass is a male donkey?"

Derek laughed.

"Is that why women call us males jerks when we've been unfriendly?"

"Weren't we talking about tails?"

"Oh, yes, and my lovely wife only puts tails on her wedding dresses."

"Derek, they are called trains, not tails. Seriously, the models will be here next week with the photographer on the yacht. Paris wants some pictures of the dresses and I thought the yacht would be a perfect white and blue backdrop."

"The yacht sounds like a great place to take a photo shoot. Will the models be wearing sheer and pom-poms?"

Jess took a large pile of the pom-poms and threw them at Derek.

"Jerk." She said the word tauntingly.

Derek took the bait.

"Jess, you shouldn't have called me a jerk. Now you'll have to pay."

"How will I have to pay?"

He grabbed the box and stuffed some pom-poms down her crop top. She started giggling and stuffed some down his shirt.

It was too much. Derek wrestled her to the floor in an embrace. Jess kept talking.

"We could put little gold chains on the pom-poms for the purse."

"Shh, no more talking."

"How about gold handcuffs."

Derek kissed her so long, she couldn't talk or breathe. Jess moaned.

Now that was what Derek wanted to hear. The zippers were opened, and he stopped when the crop-top zipper was undone. He picked up two pom-poms and put them on her eyes. Her eyes closed. His hands moved in circles and she moaned some more.

"More, please."

"Say you're sorry about calling me a jerk."

"Um, let me think about that for a while."

He kissed her some more. The tails, trains, and photo shoot were forgotten. There was no stopping their lovemaking tonight. Derek's stomach growled. He forgot to eat lunch today and he ignored the rumblings. Food could wait. Jess went limp in his arms.

Derek whispered, "I love you."

She replied, "I know, and I didn't mean it."

"I know."

He hummed a song. She recognized the tune. The song was about needing her love and her touch. The moment between them was pure heaven as their bodies combined. There was longing, and a man's wish for her love only.

The rhythm of steadfast loving lulled her senses. She was content and smiled. He was the perfect lover.

"You are a devil woman."

"A sweet devil woman?"

"I'm not sure sweet and devil work together. It's like having those pretty models wear your see-through outfit with pom-poms and not being able to touch either one."

She jabbed him in the stomach.

"Okay, I give. No more model-thought processes allowed. Yes, you're a sweet devil woman who is deliriously mine."

Derek couldn't resist.

"Fuzzy pom-pom stuff, and all."

He grabbed Jess's hands. She couldn't vent further frustration upon him.

He saw her beginning smile. The mention of give meant truce. She knew there was no one else. Derek was heavily grounded in their relationship. He wasn't going anywhere. Jess fell fast asleep in his safety and warmth.

"Ten thousand life times. Sweet dreams, honey."

Derek gently lifted her and placed her under the covers. He'd been putting her to bed for years. The song he'd been practicing for the past weeks worked too well. That was all right. He knew she'd been working hard on her designs.

He picked up the mess of pom-poms counting to forty-eight and placed them in the box. She would want them in the morning. Getting dressed, he went down to see the chef. Now he was truly starving.

"Pom-pom handcuffs. Now that's more nuts." Derek whistled as he rode their elevator.

14 Finland Detour

THE ILL MAN, Marvin Larine, placed an ad on the bulletin board in the nursing home in the hope that he could entice someone in the healthcare industry to take on the job as his caretaker.

On the opposite side of the continent, Hamm Roe lived in Montreal for over four years with Annabelle and her cousins. He was bored and tired of his relationship. Hamm told Annabelle that there was a job for him in Finland. Annabelle didn't want her husband to leave, and she argued with him.

There was no way Annabelle could sway her husband. He would send for her when there was enough money, and he felt their safety was not in jeopardy. Hamm was in Finland for three months and saw the ad. He contacted the ill man.

Taking care of the man was easy for Hamm. There was breakfast, lunch, and dinner and a few diaper changes. Marvin owned his own home and had a special bathtub with a lift device. Food was delivered once a week and a cleaning lady did the house plus laundry.

Hamm found the man's will which donated his home to some children's charity. This got Hamm to thinking that the man probably had no relatives. Opportunity stared Hamm in the face. He wondered just how he could manage changing the will to include his name first.

Conversations included the man's dying wishes and ceremonial service. Marvin told him the will was the original and he typed the document himself and went to his local bank to have the will witnessed.

Hamm brought the man's medicine from the drugstore and sat down next to the bed. The man was real ill and coughing much more. Hamm knew that the man's time was short, and he needed to take some sort of immediate action. He told him the children's charity was possibly a scam. There were rumors of impropriety with the charity funds. Hamm doctored up an article on the computer to include the charity's name to convince the ill man. Hamm finagled the man into doing a new will for a different charity. They didn't need to have the second will notarized because Hamm could color copy the other document and substitute the other charity into the document. He would blank out the signature, so Marvin could re-sign in blue ink.

Hamm prepared two different documents. The first document showed the new charity name. The second copy contained Hamm's name as the only beneficiary of Marvin's will. He let Marvin read the first copy and made the switch to the second copy for the ill man's real signature.

Marvin relaxed now that his worldly possessions were safe. The man died, and Hamm received the twenty-four thousand dollars from Marvin's estate. The old will went in the trash as did the fake charity copy.

Now that Hamm was free to go wherever he wanted, he made plans. Those plans didn't include his wife, Annabelle, who was waiting for him in Montreal with her cousins. They separated in New York six months ago. Hamm worried a brief second about the Green Stream Nevada group but read in the paper the trio were caught and placed back in jail. Their jailbreak hadn't worked with the busted gun.

Hamm grinned. "Busted. Now who's the stupid ones. Your time in jail just got extended."

Africa was a safe place now that Santan Chesin was dead. There were gold mines in Mali. Hamm Roe used his fake passport and ID. He hadn't bothered to change his name believing that no one was looking for him in Finland. He did jump a transport ship as a hired hand. They didn't check him out.

Hamm walked into the hotel bar and saw a woman eating fried food and chicken. She looked despondent. Hamm Roe was delighted. Another opportunity might be opening for him. Her badge showed that she worked at one of the mines as a tour guide. Maura was his ticket to a job at the mine, or so thought Hamm.

Mr. Hatcher was not impressed with the man. His skills at handling the heavy machinery equipment was bad at best. Mr. Hatcher recommended him to his girlfriend's business. Danielle Ashley was sent the man named Hamm Roe, to work in the packaging department. Hamm used the forklift to maneuver the shrink-wrap pallets of *XM* creams.

Hamm knew there was a private packaging room that was used whenever the owner arrived. He started to wonder about the room and began asking questions of his assistant boss. The assistant boss told him, the woman checked the packages to make sure no jars were broken, and the interior boxes were not dented or discolored.

This information grated on Hamm's logic. The woman had cheap labor that could do this job. Her checking the merchandise didn't make any sense to him. Hamm started to wonder if there was something other than cream in the copper covered jars. He found out from Maura that his boss was having an affair with two of the smartest and richest gold investors in Mali.

Hamm wondered if he could get more information out of Akash. Hamm found out that the boss was in Paris visiting her daughter. Akash let slip the boss wouldn't be around too much in the future. She would make one trip to the mine and her business. Then she would be out of the country. There was a fashion show in Paris. Akash would accompany their boss to Paris. A vacation was planned with the daughter later in Indonesia. Akash would then return to the business.

Hamm was delighted. With the boss and Akash out of the country, he could check out the special room. This wasn't the first time he had searched a place. If anything was hidden, he felt sure that his smarts would find deceptive products or activities.

15   Psychologist in Miami

RHONDA PETERS WAS sitting with Tami Cortez in a café in Miami. They were waiting for a psychologist to arrive. Rhonda placed the manila package on the table.

Rosemary Quinn sat down at their table.

"Hello, girls. Isn't this lovely? It's too cold to eat outside in Cape Cod. That's the reason why I escape to Miami. So, tell me what the problem is you have with a police issue. There's something about an elusive female. Tami informed me of what's in your folder."

Rhonda signaled the waiter to take Rosemary's order. Once he left, Rhonda slid over the folder.

"This is an updated copy of what we currently have on the person we call Snake woman. We hope there might be something in the file regarding her personality that we might have missed. Our hope is that your professional insight might light some sparks under our investigation. We're at a hard stop."

Rosemary nodded. "Tami asked if I knew a person by the name of Matin Domingo from Miami. She knows my ex-husband has a second firm here and one in Los Angeles. I personally am not going to approach my ex-husband, but I do know some of his friends at the firm. They may also know something about Mr. Burrows, the former lawyer for Matin. Men usually talk at lunch about their current dealings with clients. Anyway, it's worth a shot."

Rhonda said, "We've already tried that approach and gotten nothing."

"Well, with me, things might be different because I'm part of their little group, even though I'm divorced. They may divulge more information to me."

"Okay, fair enough." Rhonda sipped her water and swirled the lemon rind.

Tami perked up. "You can call me if there are any questions about the split-personality in that folder. She's like fifty personalities rolled into one."

Rosemary visibly brightened. "I love when women are outspoken regarding other women. You think this Snake woman has a split personality? She could very well have the symptoms which would be someone's first guess."

"I also would like a list of her weaknesses."

"Weaknesses? With a hired assassin who has successfully maintained her freedom, I would call them strengths. Let me explain. I worked for two years as a prison psychologist. Enlightenment comes to mind at a high rate of speed working with caged people. There was one person who stood out. He was a hired assassin like the snake person. Murder was important. The planning, however, was the ultimate thrill. He told me about the hours of memorizing the minutest detail. It was those hours of work that mattered. He agreed, and we took a test of his IQ. His intelligence was off the charts and the highest I've ever seen. The man had total recall abilities. He could remember names, places, streets in cities. He was his own built-in GPS system."

Rosemary sipped her lemon water.

"I tried to compare him to Maslow's self-actualizing personality traits which boils down to a person's growth to the highest need. It's motivation-based theory, or knowledge and intelligence fully aware. He was fully aware of himself except there was no morality involved. He was flawed in that there was only one thing in his pyramid, the top layer which was the self without judgment. Yet, he knew right from wrong. Most of us carry a real self and ideal self. With him, the ideal person was his only self-reigning, supreme being. There's where the words split personality hang up. A real self never appeared in his personality. This man and your criminal are an anomaly. Consequently, the police cannot catch your Snake woman because they are using old theories."

Rhonda bristled, "That's a bunch of riddles. We have the best technology out there to catch criminals."

Rosemary sighed. Rhonda was getting defensive. The two women weren't getting the picture.

"Okay, I'm not explaining this in layman's terms. Your Snake woman is more than one of a kind. There are layers and layers to her personality. Each layer allows her to hide. How do I know this? I saw this man upfront, close, and personal. He seems exactly like her. He has the same layer-ability. The most important layer is the top. For your suspect, the mirror is only her. That is all there is. On occasion, *something else shows in the mirror*. A child or lover could penetrate the barrier she has erected. Now, you're thinking where did the barrier come from? Her past shows trauma which changed the personality. Maybe a parent was too strict or rigid. She was adopted by scientists. She learned to become shrewd and hide. Her intelligence at age two must have shown. Perhaps people took advantage of her skills. Hence, the barrier keeps people out."

Rosemary looked at two women listening intently, but not understanding.

"I found difficulty understanding how the police were able to capture my guy. The point that I'm trying to make is this person is a fearless loner. There is only him. However, he trusted someone else to make an important decision for him. That is how he became locked up. The self for a moment became real. This Snake woman will make an error, eventually. She will become real and trust someone again. Therein, lies her exposure. Whether the police will catch her is debatable. She is adaptable."

Rhonda said, "We understand the loner and see this in her makeup. Our closeness to our suspect has taught us everything we see in our report. Highly intelligent, absolutely. We have figured out already her degree of knowledge because of her scientific experiments with poison, using the mamba snake. The planning idea was there, but you are putting heavy significance to the planning. In other words, you're saying she is a mastermind. She would make a good reconnaissance person for a country in their special operation forces."

"Yes, Rhonda. Reconnaissance and resilience with a capital R. Reconnaissance is small stuff for her. Her mind and caginess show brilliance. Her ability to bounce and land correctly amazes me. Most people break and take years to mend. Not her. You have a police report showing only her surface or what she wants you to see. You truly must understand who she is. She's the ultimate woman. She is one classy, super girl."

"Ouch, we wouldn't list her that way. You make her sound nice. Trust me, she is a savage person who destroys."

Rosemary thought further.

"Other countries have figured her out. They aren't interested in catching her. She gets rid of their garbage or savages. She does the job neatly and efficiently, I might add. The countries aren't smart enough to offer her a job because the woman scares the crap out of them. They don't know how to handle her. I hope someday, our side figures this dilemma and offers her a job."

"We're trying to catch her, not immortalize the woman. You are talking craziness. She is wanted for murder."

"And our operatives kill who we want them to kill. *We ask them to murder and don't care who's crazy*. We want to win and make allowances. Those allowances tell them to break the rules if needed. Next, we hide the truth or act like we have no knowledge. Survival is one of the purest concepts. Survival is the ideal self that makes the world turn.

Even animals acknowledge ideal self. There's no difference between our operatives and your Snake woman."

Tami said, "Now girls, I think we need to come to a truce."

Rosemary couldn't resist one parting shot at the recognition of their dilemma.

"You, however, have been able to get close. She could have killed you. But you were an accidental meet, and you weren't any part of her current game plan. She didn't need to kill you to survive. The situation was quickly assessed by her. That's the only reason she has left you and Derek alive. The woman controls her environment. Every move is monitored. Besides, you've not been invited to the Snake dance."

Rhonda looked upset by the closing comments of their interview.

Rosemary softened. Perhaps she had been too harsh.

"I know that I haven't read your police report. I do read the newspapers and have followed what I can about this strange assassin. The similarities that I see with this other prisoner and your Snake woman leave me to wonder if they aren't, somehow, related. The prisoner that I know has blocked out his past. The void is deep. He goes catatonic when I question him. The prison has tried to control his reaction by giving him drugs. Most incarcerated prisoners like to talk. This man isn't normal in his environment. The problem he has in the prison is the inability to escape. He's locked up for life. Catatonic is his way to escape now. The other thing that bothers me is what he mentioned before he went catatonic. I haven't had the time to research the group. He said the name, *Comet*."

Tami and Rhonda both looked up. They both caught the words: related and comet.

Rhonda said, "Why, catatonic escape? There must be someone who can talk to him. Drugs might be too much and affect his memory. Do you have the name of the prisoner and his prison location? We might want to visit him."

"I do and will be glad to write down the information for you. Good luck on getting him to talk with you. His health is failing. I've kept in contact with one of his guards at the prison."

Rhonda did a paper while in her police academy training. The thesis was on American sub-terrorists. Rhonda called them substitutes because their actions hadn't killed people. They practiced a lot in the woods and kept to themselves. The hatred was mild compared to other groups. The police watched them because they felt there was a spark that could flame at any time in this group. Rhonda was familiar with the other various groups in the area.

"Comet was a group of men and women who originally lived in Oregon. The leader, Jackson Remy, was a retired special ops man who somehow went astray. He developed issues from overwork in his field. The government allowed him to be dishonorably discharged. His intelligence was high, and it was a shame to lose him. You think this man in prison is one of his offspring?"

"That's why I mentioned him. You can better research his background."

Rhonda tried to digest the information.

"There could be a connection between your prisoner and our suspect. That's interesting. If true, our Snake woman grew up in an American terrorist camp. They trained their children at an early age from survival techniques to tactical warfare."

Tami was confused and said, "What did comet stand for?"

Rhonda said, "Heavy-duty stuff, we call them cosmic frozen gas. No, I'm being facetious. The word means coordinated organization of men engaged in terrorism."

Rosemary handed the note of the prisoner's name to Rhonda.

"His name is David Remy, and he is now in a jail in Phoenix for some other crimes committed there."

Rhonda pocketed the name.

"Also, one last idea about your Snake woman. Her mind rolls to walking on the wilder side and very close to danger. Danger represents normalcy. The danger doesn't matter. There's no effect on her psyche. An example would be a person exposed to a flame. Normal people feel the heat and pull back. She doesn't feel anything and walks through the flame. The flame doesn't hurt her. There's no cognizance of danger nor does she care. Her experience tells her to keep going. Her ideal self knows she can make it to the other side. Once on the other side, she takes a break. She enjoys the walk on a pretty beach. It's part of her recovery plan before the next plan or project."

Tami sipped her drink and shook her head in amazement.

Rosemary glanced at the restaurant kitchen door and saw her waiter.

"Let me categorize her strengths in the order of importance as I see them. I'll put that at the beginning of my report. It will take me about three weeks if that is all right. I want to enjoy my vacation first."

"No problem with vacation. Please send the report back to Derek's office," said Rhonda.

The waiter brought Rosemary's lunch and the girls talked about current fashion designs, celebrities, and good makeup techniques. The thought of suspects and personality differences was quickly forgotten.

Rosemary would create her list and send the report to Derek. There were very private notes she sent to herself about Snake woman. Those notes included the person as highly motivated to infiltrate any government she chose. The Snake person had massive avenues at her disposal. There was no way to catch her. The walls surrounding her were impenetrable.

Derek would read the first page of Snake woman's strengths that the psychologist prepared. The order of the list made no sense to him and the arrows threw him off. He hadn't heard about the prisoner or the rest of the women's conversation. Rhonda would later fill him in.

Derek ran his fingers through his hair, the diagram bothered him. Somewhere he had seen this line diagram, but he couldn't remember the object or place. He would have to ask Rhonda. Women's brains were heavy into details. His wife could remember entire conversations that happened years ago.

Major Strengths:

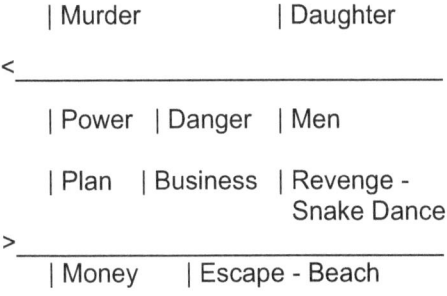

Derek would stop reading the report because he believed the psychologist was wrong in her assessment of Snake woman's strengths. He would have pegged them as weaknesses. The diagram wasn't helpful, and he wondered how much they paid for the report.

"Probably too much."

He would not read the rest of the report until later. The report was placed in his out basket.

Derek would miss *something*.

16   Danielle's Return

BEFORE DANIELLE ASHLEY returned, Hamm proposed to Maura. They quickly got married and Hamm took a short break on his honeymoon. When he came back to work, there was a note on his locker that the boss wanted to speak to him after his shift.

He sweated a little bit about meeting the boss for the first time but saw the location of the meeting. The place was her special room where she checked the merchandise. Hamm was ebullient. He would volunteer to do this for her, so she would be free to run other aspects of her business.

Hamm entered the room. The woman was talking with Akash. Slowly, Danielle turned around. Her eyes turned almost black. Hamm stepped back a few feet and then got a grip. He hurried forward with his hand extended. Ashley ignored the hand.

"Sit down, Mr. Roe, or is your name really Stew Avery?"

Hamm's mouth dried up like a shrunken prune. He tried to speak and then he looked at the door. Akash had moved to block any escape.

Hamm stumbled to the chair and sat down. The glow from his honeymoon weekend quickly wore off. The boss knew who he was and his background. He wondered if he was going to get fired. Africa wasn't looking so good as a place to hide out after all. Hamm kept his mouth shut.

Danielle grew impatient. "You haven't answered my question?"

Hamm couldn't remember the question. "Oh, yes. My background on the resume was probably a little incorrect or maybe a huge mistake. I'm sure you can understand my reasoning. There are people who don't like me very much. I'm not sure why. Somehow, I found myself in prison. There were no crimes too big when you look at the whole picture. Gold was involved, and I do love gold. You love gold cause you are here in Africa and wear gold all the time. The allure is overpowering. It is hard to ignore money." Hamm ran out of words.

The boss lady came around and sat on her desk.

"You married someone this weekend."

"Yes, yes, I did. She's a tour guide at Mr. Hatcher's mine."

"Does Maura Dane have an infinity for gold or does she snoop into other people's business?"

Hamm couldn't believe that his boss hit things right on the nail head. He wondered if she was psychic?

"No, no, she isn't crazy like I am about gold, but she likes the tourists and sometimes follows them out of curiosity."

"Curious people don't live too long in this country."

Now Hamm knew he was in trouble.

"Please don't turn me into the officials here. Their prison system is not too deluxe."

"You would rather go back to Los Angeles?"

Hamm visibly cringed thinking about Annabelle and the Green Stream gang.

"Look, I'll do anything for you. I don't want to go to jail and especially LA."

Danielle looked at Akash.

"We could use one more person because the shipments have risen," said Akash.

"Hamm, you will be trained by Akash from now on. You will not run the forklift. There will be an increase in pay. The amount will be twice your current salary. You owe me your allegiance. No one will know anything about my business or else. Do you understand the exchange we made today?"

Hamm was surprised. He received a new job with more pay and obviously, more responsibility.

"Yes, I understand perfectly. Can I take off and tell my new bride?"

Akash said, "Of course, we can start tomorrow. There will be much work to do. Save your energy because the next few days will be long. We work until we are done with the shipment."

"Okay, I'll be back tomorrow on time."

Danielle waved, "Tell your wife to be careful and she should stay out of the hotel bar."

"I will do that very thing."

Hamm quickly exited the room. Tomorrow would come soon enough. He bought some beer and ready-made chicken sandwiches to take home. It was time to celebrate his new job. He couldn't believe he told her about the gold objects. He still remembered how beautiful the antique staff looked when they stole it from the Wrights. Wouldn't his cousin be surprised how much money he was going to make in Africa. He almost contacted his cousin, but then thought better of it. The police might still have his cousin's phone tapped. His cousin still owned a land line. He didn't know his cousin moved to Mexico.

What Hamm also didn't know was that he had stepped into the lion's den, or snake pit. Recovery from his misstep would depend on his decision-making abilities. Making right decisions were not his strong points in the past.

The new shipment of gold arrived at Danielle's place of business for packaging in the morning. The gold was smuggled from a mine in the area.

17   Paris Preparation

JESS CHECKED OFF her last shipment of dresses, pant suits, bags, shoes, and jewelry that were being sent to the Paris Fashion Week warehouse. The boys at the Wright warehouse came to pick up the pallets for delivery at the Los Angeles docks.

She went back inside to the small kitchen, grabbed her salad and juice, and went to the library where her notebook computer sat. There were a few more items she wanted to order for their Christmas decorations. She contacted the manager of a silver company and chatted a while with him. The company could handle making the mold for her designs. The items would be complete in time for her special date.

The Christmas tree and decorations were ordered. She put a note on Derek's calendar to notify the captain of their yacht about the shipment and the date the lights should be placed on the yacht.

Checking her watch, she closed her computer and placed the item in her bag. It was time to pick up their twin girls from school. She would need to order presents when she arrived home.

The preparation for the Paris show had taken weeks and weeks of her time. Rhonda, Tami, Tami's husband Cortez and his brother were going to the show this year as her protection squad. Derek would fly in later to the show to join her. At the last minute Tiare Palla decided to attend. Ara and Jack Jones couldn't make it because they were babysitting the Wright twin girls.

Jess felt confident in her designs for the show. She began to relax. The company always chose designer of the year before the show started. She hoped she would place in the top five. Her colors for her outfits reflected space and the moon or stars. There was a new color out called ultra-violet and very shiny fabric.

She ordered a sample and didn't like the color or the way the fabric clung. Jess didn't want to use the static spray at the show. Clingy fabric didn't work well with a model's legs. The fabric was dropped from her color scheme.

According to the brochure, several designers chose the color in their lineup of gowns. The runway would be saturated with ultra-violet. She could see the judges must have quickly become bored with the same hue. Only one designer went the extra mile to create a fresh evening gown. Her designs won first place. Jess liked her choice in creating curves and slits in exotic places. Jess won second place and was content. Her designs would be presented second at the show and give her an edge for the larger vendors who purchased her designs.

The special gear from the Space company arrived. There was a watch and bracelet that contained a tiny chip. The chip was a tracking device in case she was separated from the group. The Space company warned Derek the devices might not work if they got wet or were underground. Both would mess with the signal.

A new bodyguard would meet them in Paris for the duration of the show. The police would be notified of their arrival because Derek would be packing a gun as would their protection team. The limousines were ordered from a large company in Paris to take the Wrights and their people to the show from the hotel, plus any entertainment, and local restaurants.

Jess attended the Paris show for three years prior and knew all the commotion surrounding the runway. There would be lots of patrons, celebrities, and rich people. Photographers were in abundance and the news media.

The word, *chaos*, came into her mind. She didn't dare tell Derek this word. It would scare him off.

18   Paris Fashion Show

THE BODYGUARD INTRODUCED himself at their hotel. His name was Jerome Dupre, and he joined Jess in the limousine to the grand entrance of the Paris Fashion Show. The red-carpeted path was used to guide them inside where Jess was greeted by the coordinator.

She was immediately taken backstage to view her hanging wardrobe to ensure the items were safe and in the correct order. The models were waiting to put their outfits on for her as a preview. A short inner runway had been created specifically for the designers.

Jess noticed a jar of cream on one of the model's dressing table. She opened the copper top of the jar and smelled. Her model came back to get her powder for one last dab to subdue the shine.

"Isn't this a lovely smell. The designer and manufacturer were new this year to the show. As a gift, all the models received a jar in their welcome bag."

Jess looked at the jar again, read the ingredients, and saw the place of manufacture.

"Africa, how odd?"

A slight chill touched her hand. Some misgivings about the show flickered across her mind. Derek wouldn't be happy. She wondered about the designer.

"*XM*, what a strange cream name? X was sometimes written as an expression of love. Then there was the M. Derek told her about the Snake woman case. The name Margaret and Matin jumped off the report page when she read it. But then so had the word Shannen. Jess shook her head. She was reading too much into things. She must leave the police case off her thoughts during this trip to Paris.

Jess stepped back to let the model finish her makeup. The fragrance smell filled her nostrils. Jess coughed.

The bodyguard took his place in the small grouping of audience chairs. The bodyguard was glad that this gig included beautiful women. He was enjoying the show.

The show finally started. The audience was packed. Music was by Heat Fantasy, a new London hard rock band, with swirls of drums, staccato, and heavy sound. The models were excited and danced backstage before their turn on the runway. Jess called Derek.

"Hi, sweetheart, are you there?"

"What is all the racket?"

Jess tried to explain.

"I can tell you are having a good time, Jess. I'll call you this evening at your hotel when it's sane to talk with you." Derek rung off.

Jess turned back to the fashion show. The models walked and danced the runway in their finery. Their walk was elegance and beauty in motion. The fabrics flared and fluttered from their movement and the low fans imbedded on the side of the runway.

Each designer's collection was unique, and the colors vibrated the senses. The heated passion of designer world came through in hot gowns. The music intensified the solar degrees. There were many camera shots of the main stage which elevated the temperature even further. There was no need for oil spray or glitter makeup on the model's bodies. Their own aura shone through. Happiness was an elevated high. The audience caught on fast. Emotional was the scene with the audience dancing during the halfway mark. The first day was a major sell-out. Money exchanged hands. Orders flowed. News spread, and all the rest of the fashion show ticket seats sold out in five minutes when they saw the lead singer of the band. Hunk was a soft word to describe him.

Jess would be photographed with her models and collection. One photographer caught a model in her collection twirling with Jess rocking to the band's beat. The picture went viral. The crony families and Derek's friends helped push the shot.

All the designers would repeat the same photographic session. The photographs would hit the newspapers. One designer would be showcased more than the others.

For two days, they did the familiar scene. Derek would arrive this evening to attend the last show. Jess and her bodyguard were at the after-show party put on by the coordinators and sponsors. The players were dressed to the nines, very high class.

The models mingled in their last outfits from the runway. They wore evening gowns. Jess smiled and did a high five across the room to her model. The gown wore bands of open stars between white and gold lame strips in the skirt. The top was a halter crisscross of dark navy-blue velvet. Her heels were gold and navy sling style with clear heels. A white star joined the front strap of the heel. A plain velvet clutch accompanied the ensemble. The diamond necklace was shaped into a star, especially custom created and paid for by Derek. The necklace was her present from him for obtaining her ticket into the designer world at the show.

Jess had chosen not to wear a necklace this evening as the model would hand the star necklace over to her before leaving. The necklace would go perfect with her topaz earrings and topaz silk dress. The dress had long sleeves and a scarf around the neck with gold stars. Her jacket was a light woven wool and silk blend in topaz and black. She chose the fabric because the night air in Paris in December was chilly. Her fur coat was in the cloak room along with the bodyguard's overcoat.

Jess and her bodyguard went to the buffet tables to get a quick bite before re-mingling with the crowd. She ate a small slider open face sandwich, hot cheese balls, and Asian lettuce wraps. The bodyguard brought her a glass of champagne. She sipped the bubbly drink slowly and scanned the bright assemblage of people. The room appeared filled to maximum capacity. The bodyguard and Jess decided to take the stairwell down to the next floor which wasn't quite so full.

In the stairwell, Jess saw a finely dressed woman with a man who, obviously was a bodyguard or escort for the evening. Next, the man turned.

Jess breathed inward. She couldn't believe who she saw. She told her bodyguard that they must follow the couple because Jess knew the man. They raced down the stairs as a limousine approached. The color of the limo was not the same as their hired company. Jess called out, "Stew."

The man turned around, and a large gun came out. The woman also took a gun out of her handbag, shielding her weapon from the street camera.

"Get in the car."

The bodyguard looked at Jess. There was no one at this side exit. The cars went past the opening too fast to hitch a ride.

The woman searched Jess's bodyguard and took his gun. She grabbed Jess's purse. The bodyguard and Jess stepped inside the limousine. Jess touched her watch to activate the tracking device. The woman saw the move and made Jess remove her bracelet, watch, and blue topaz earrings. The woman threw the items out the window along with metal piece the bodyguard wore.

They arrived at an old warehouse building and went down two floors in an elevator. Jess counted the Bing sound as the buttons were totally worn off with no numbers showing. They were placed in two separate jail cells. There were only two cells, two cots, and two sinks with toilet. The camera looked new in the corner. Old woolen blankets adorned the cots. Jess turned to ask her captors a question.

The woman and Stew already left.

The bodyguard was frustrated. "Now, what do we do?"

Jess sat down on her cot.

"Right now, we wait. I'm thinking ransom money."

"And who is this Stew person?"

"A rat and weasel." It was the only way to describe the man.

"I'm glad we ate and drank something. Does the water work?"

"Mine doesn't. Go try yours," said Jess.

"Nothing. I suppose the toilets are the same thing. Maybe we can ask for water if they come back."

The bodyguard was silent. Jess grew silent. It would be a long night. She knew Derek would be frantic upon arrival when Rhonda met him at the airport. The police were already working the scene when they found the two winter coats were left in the coat room. Tami and the Cortez brothers stopped watching Jess for a few seconds. They were distraught and notified Rhonda and Tiare. A search of the floors showed nothing. The street camera would reveal when they disappeared. No one knew where Stew or Hamm took her. The older woman was no one they knew.

A day went by with no food or water. The woman finally appeared. She passed a bag with a sandwich and two bottles of water to each one.

Jess said, "Why have you detained us? Don't you know who I am?"

The woman replied, "I do. You are Jess Wright. Somehow, we accidentally crossed paths. Believe me, this incident was unexpected and unfortunate."

"Why unfortunate? You will let us go. My husband will search for me."

"I believe you."

"My husband is very powerful, and we have many friends. There is no place that you can hide."

"On the contrary, there are many places in this world where I can hide. I see that you don't know who I am."

Jess smelled the fragrance. The woman was the designer and manufacturer of the cream at the fashion show.

"There's a word that your husband calls me. It is Snake woman."

The bodyguard came closer to the jail bars. Jess's eyes grew a deeper blue-gray. She remembered Dean Crain, her old friend and confidante. He told her to *show no fear*.

"I don't care who you are. I have done nothing wrong or hurt you."

The Snake woman was surprised at the lack of fear. Derek chose his woman wisely. She was a strong one.

"Tell your husband to stop tracking me. I don't have time for his interruptions into my life."

"He won't stop."

Snake woman was even more surprised by her answer.

"Then he will pay."

That was the moment Jess had been waiting for. She knew armies of people were looking for her. This woman wasn't going to scare the crap out of her. Nor would she let the woman endanger her family.

"Be careful how you speak. A woman will fight to the death. If you kill one, another will appear. We are sisters. Sisters, cousins, and more will join. There won't be an end. War will happen. Is that what you want for your daughter?"

The Snake woman regretted ever reading her Tracker's journal. Her next victims were to be Rich Madden and Jess Wright. The hits were never ordered by her. No one knew those facts. The Tracker accomplished one of her death wishes. Rich Madden no longer existed. The fact that Snake woman intervened was an Ace-card she would keep for now. Jess Wright hadn't been murdered. This was not an appropriate time to reveal her bad employee to anyone.

Snake woman wanted to meet Jess although she didn't plan on doing the meet this way. Derek was an interesting sparring partner. She meant neither him or his wife ill-will. She felt a connection somehow to his woman. She was impressed with Jess. She was also impressed with Derek's crude attempts to capture her.

The Snake woman backed away from Jess.

"A mother elephant does a trumpet call to scare predators and to bring her pack back to help protect her baby. I like you Jess Wright, and you will have your freedom soon."

Snake woman stopped and turned back.

"*You're lucky.*"

The captor walked out the door. They could hear the elevator motor as the cab ascended.

Jess didn't know the mother-sister theme hit a nerve. Plus, the mere mention of Snake woman's daughter gave Jess the ticket to her freedom. There were confusing crossfires in the Snake woman. Jess felt something was wrong in their estimation or police profile.

"I know I'm lucky," said Jess to herself. This was her defensive move. She held Derek's love close to her heart for protection. The meeting with Snake woman unnerved her.

The prisoner release would happen in two days. The Snake woman needed the time to escape. The bomb on the door was to open the facility so they could escape. An escape was imminent. The Snake woman didn't know Hamm would interfere and change her well-laid plans.

The bodyguard looked at Jess and she lifted her eyes.

"Geez, what did I get into here?"

Jess laughed. It felt good to be strong for the moment.

"A small war."

Jerome hated to think this was small in his employer's eyes. The scene looked major to him.

She opened her sandwich and drank the water. Jess sat for a long time thinking. She slid her hand along the metal cot. A bar fell loose in her hand. She took off her scarf and wrapped the object in it. She crossed over to Jerome. He took the piece. Jess nodded to the corner where the camera couldn't see.

Her bodyguard noticed the decay in the wall. The structure was not all concrete. There was wood in the corner. Jerome nodded. He would work all night and place the dirt under his blanket. They might get out. He needed time.

19   The Search

THE INVESTIGATOR FROM Los Angeles arrived at the police station.

"Mr. Wright, we are so sorry to hear about your wife's disappearance. We have our best people searching for her."

Derek solemnly said, "Show me exactly where you are searching for her."

After three hours, he was driven to his and Jess's hotel room.

Rhonda came over immediately. Derek was pacing the room and rubbing his hands through his brown hair.

"We'll find her."

"I don't know, Rhonda. I'm worried. We saw the tape of her and Jerome getting in the limousine with the woman and Stew or Hamm. Little did I believe that we would see him again. We found Annabelle and she told us that her husband, Hamm, went to Finland. She hadn't heard from him in nine months. The police have put her in jail for aiding and abetting his escape. Randy Moore posted her bail."

"Someone recognized the woman as the designer of a woman's cream. The police in Mali have been contacted to research her place of business. But that still leaves Jess missing. We have no idea why this woman would take her, much less go into some business with Hamm."

Derek spread the map on the hotel desk.

"Here are the areas the police have searched and the ones they will do tomorrow."

Rhonda pointed to the area that her team would attack.

"If I were a kidnaper, I'd pick a warehouse."

"Then, let's search the warehouses first. Make sure you are with Tami and the Cortez brothers. If something goes south, they are the best of our group to have on board. I have sent Tiare home for now."

Rhonda made a motion to leave, came back, and hugged Derek.

"Jess will keep her cool wherever she is."

"I know. I'm the one who would like to kill Hamm Roe for this new disaster. Jess only followed him to stop whatever his new plans were. There must be money involved. I mentioned to the police that we need to track the designer's money trail."

"That's great. Goodnight, Derek."

Derek received a call from the Captain of their yacht in Los Angeles.

"There's a package for Jess and she put me on the copy of the note."

Derek pulled up his calendar.

"Hold off on the Christmas lights. I can't deal with the yacht now."

"But Jess loves the bright."

Derek told him, "No lights."

The phone call ended. Derek thumped on the map.

"Where would a rat and snake hide?"

XXXXXX

Hamm brought food on two trays in the morning for the bodyguard and Jess. He placed the trays on the floor. The food was hot and smelled good. He was supposed to pick the sandwiches from this special store for the prisoners. Hamm was lazy and selected take-out from a closer restaurant. He could go to the back door to get the trays.

He stopped by the outside door. Lightly tapping the box, he tried to peer under the object. The box wasn't there yesterday. He was sure the device was new. The wires ran down the molding to the door knob and lock.

"A bomb? Seriously."

Hamm began to sweat. He didn't see any electrical wires going into the wall.

"Looks like a remote to me. Darn it. This woman is crazy. Maybe I should walk away. No, there's Maura. Danielle knows where to find her. Let me think."

Hamm picked up the trays, rode the elevator, and slid them one by one under the jail bars.

Jess came to the jail cell door.

"Let us out, Hamm."

Hamm backed away.

"No, I can't. She will come after me and my wife."

"Annabelle, you told her about your wife."

Hamm stopped.

"Not Annabelle."

"Wait, don't go. You must contact the police. Can't you see how important our escape would be? I can put in a good word when they put you back in prison."

It was no use, Hamm left. He didn't want to help the Wrights in any way, shape, or form. He was glad Jess was locked up with her bodyguard. Jail was her sentence for finding the sunken treasure off Dakar. The treasure should have been his. There was no way he wanted to be reminded of prison. They were so stupid. He could have thrown their meal away. No one would have been the wiser.

The prisoners ate their meal of hot beef soup. Jess saved her water for later, eating the roll with butter.

Later in the day, Jess smelled smoke.

"There's smoke in the building."

Jerome stopped his carving at the wood and crumbling wall. The smoke was coming through the hole he made. He didn't think that he carved through a wire. He would have felt a jolt of electricity. Grabbing his lightweight jacket, he stuffed the soft wool into the hole. The smoke diminished a small amount.

"I think we need to prepare ourselves. I'm not sure how fast the fire department will come. It's good that they will arrive except we need to stay alive."

Jess worried about Snake woman. Smoke wasn't her style at all. She couldn't believe setting a fire was Hamm's either.

The air looked gray in the room. The smell grew stronger. There were no sirens. She strained to hear. She heard her bodyguard praying.

"Shouldn't we try to go through the opening? I'm smaller. I might be able to make it out."

The hole was partially on her side of the wall.

"No. We don't know what's out there. The elevator may not work, and we don't know where the stairs are located. I know it's getting hot, but the heat could be worse outside these walls. Get down as close to the floor as you can. Pull the cot over."

His logic made sense. All she wanted was to be home with Derek and her family. Jess wrapped herself in the blanket and pulled her cot over. She poured water on her scarf to hold over the mouth and nose. She held her breath and tried not to breathe. Skid had worked with her a long time when they were practicing for dives. He told her sometimes a diver can't count on their air tank. Jess heard his voice coaching her in their sessions about panic. If you panic, you breathe faster and deeper which is what you do not want to do in a limited oxygen environment. The first thing that you must learn is to relax and control your breathing. In their diving sessions, the oxygen tank was readily available. She wished she had one. Jess made her body relax.

"I'll have to come to America to see you. Thank you for inviting me to your next party."

Jerome coughed and pulled his blanket over his torso.

"You're welcome."

Jess eyes stung, and she coughed. It was time to stop talking. The smoke was deeper. She thought she heard Dean's number seven song from their yacht.

Jess said, "Dean?"

There was no response. She heard Dean and Louisa talking to her. She missed her dear friend, Dean, and Louisa Renaliere. Dean shouted that she wasn't a ghost. She must go back. Louisa nodded agreement. The images blurred.

Jess remembered the ghost restaurant in San Francisco. She wondered where she should go back. She was confused. What happened after the ghosts? She couldn't remember. It was useless. She reconciled to herself that she was prepared to die. Her breathing slowed.

Dean shouted again. He told her to fight. She thought about her life flashing past her in glimpses. She saw Derek. That's why she should fight. Dean and Louisa were right. She must go back. Derek was waiting for her. Jess prayed.

Finally, she could hear the fire engine horn. Jess held her breath a few more times, poured the last of her water on the face cloth, and waited. She could hear voices. The voices seemed closer. The elevator started. Jess was back in the building. This was the correct place. There was no more good air. Her lungs couldn't find any. She saw darkness and blacked out. The bodyguard was already unconscious.

20   Fire Run

THE FIREMEN QUICKLY extinguished the flames before the fire could run any further on the one floor, and they started the search of the building.

The fire master called the police.

"We need the bomb squad here fast. One of the doors has a device."

Rhonda and her crew saw the fire in the distance. They were in the next district.

Cortez said, "Let's go check out the fire. Something strange is happening in this city."

Tami voiced her opinion.

"You and your brother go see what has happened. Rhonda and I will stay here. Call us on the radio if there are any problems. Take the car because it will be faster. We'll talk to the owner of this building first. We should be done by the time you get back."

"Okay, love, we'll follow your orders. See you later. I like it when you try to boss me around."

"Go, just go." She gave her husband a gentle shove.

The Cortez brothers were watching the police unload the bomb-finding robot when Cortez looked at the group of spectators that gathered on the street.

There was a man closely watching the firemen and bomb squad. Cortez signaled to his brother. They were going to approach the man for information.

Hamm turned to look directly at the two brothers when he realized they were part of the Miami crony family that Derek Wright worked with. Cortez suddenly recognized the perp and yelled, "Hey you, stop where you are." His brother took out his silver badge Derek gave him one year for Christmas and he waved it in the air. Hamm started running.

His brother yelled into the phone letting Rhonda and Tami know they were on a chase. Their suspect, Hamm Roe, was running on foot. Rhonda and Tami had the police drop them off at the warehouse. They wanted to walk the floors with the firemen after the bomb squad was done. Derek was alerted across town and was on his way to the smoking warehouse. He thought about Jess and quickly dismissed the probability of her being at the fire location.

Hamm was running for his life. This was not a good idea for him to return to the warehouse. This was a wrong move and not his day. He rolled under a parked truck and lifted the manhole cover. Slipping quickly into the darkness, rats came out the top.

Cortez arrived next to the truck and caught his breath.

"There isn't any possible way that I'm going down this rat hole. I'm deathly afraid of rats."

Rhonda heard him say the last sentence from the brother's phone. She couldn't help but suppress a laugh.

"Tell him he has to go. That's an order."

His brother replied, "I'll go if he'll move his body out of my way." He shoved Cortez aside and crawled under the truck. Two more rats came scurrying out. Cortez looked down the street and saw

Hamm climb out of the next manhole. More rats came streaming out.

"The perp's out on the street running again. No need for the sewer connection."

Cortez followed Hamm north. His brother took the side street to create a circular surround. They hoped he would keep moving in the same direction, so the brother could run into him.

Cortez stopped and couldn't figure where the man went. His brother came around the corner. They stood by the bus stop. A young girl waiting with her mother pointed at the bus. Cortez saw him.

"Thank you, sweetheart."

They crossed the busy traffic as the bus pulled away.

"He's on the bus, number 40, is on the back metal plate. We need a car. We're on Rue de something. The sign is bent."

Tami came around the corner with her rental car.

"How did you find me?"

"Get in, silly, the tracker in your watch kicked in. You must have accidentally turned it on."

The car raced after the bus and Hamm saw them from the back window. He moved to the front and the bus pulled over to the next stop. Both men jumped out of the car.

Suddenly, there was screaming as Hamm pulled out his gun. People flew out the back door creating congestion the brothers were forced to move through.

Hamm made it to the next corner and the police car was waiting for him. Turning back, he ran through the alley. Cortez and his brother were in close pursuit. His brother grabbed a bike chain sticking out of one of the garbage bins and threw it. The chain lassoed in the air and wrapped around Hamm's leg pulling him down. His arms grabbed onto a garbage bin with a black plastic bag. The bag broke and cat litter with excrement poured onto Hamm. The black cat jumped off the other garbage bin and scratched Hamm across the brow.

Cortez used the nylon ties to secure their prisoner for the police. He called Tami and she told him they found Jess in the warehouse. The ambulance crew were taking care of her, and Tami would be on the way to their location.

His brother smiled. "Did you hear that chain do rat-a-tat-tat before it hit him?"

Cortez shook his head.

"Did you have to say rat!"

"Well, look at the man. Is there something I missed?"

"Yeah, cat-a-rat-a-rat-a."

"Now that's a good one."

Now that their prisoner was secured, it was time to relax. Cortez started dancing and twirling to his favorite pop song. The music was playing on his phone. He moved his feet in a thriller-type dance. His brother pretended to play the drums. They went crazier when they heard the police sirens. They were shaking to their internal rhythm, and people started filling the alleyway watching the two-man dance machine. The gathering clapped to the men's beat, giving their approval. The acoustic sound drew a larger crowd. The people read the Paris papers and knew someone was captured in their alleyway. There was no way this person was going to escape.

The brother's danced side by side with perfect precision, matching the funky beat-a-beat noise. They had been practicing their routine for a dance at the Wright's annual party. Now that they saw their audience, it was showtime.

Someone videotaped the dance on their phone and would later upload the dance on the internet. The Cortez brothers would again be a sensation. This time they would have celebrity status in Paris. The flight attendants would offer them free lunch and drinks on their flight home to Miami.

This commotion was too much for Hamm. He was tired of Cortez and his brother's chatter. The crowd scared him. He thought about mob-mentality. Hamm wanted no part of the creepy crowd from Paris. He hated being there in the first place.

"Do you have a tissue or something? This stuff is revolting."

Cortez said, "Revolting. Nah, this is a wee bit of dirt." He grabbed the other black bag and showed it to the crowd. They all cheered. Cortez walked over to the person who was doing the video.

"Hey, mate, can you give us a break. We need a moment with our prisoner."

The man turned off his machine.

Cortez tore a hole and poured the mess on Hamm.

His brother said, "Now that's revolting."

The crowd separated, and the police arrived which allowed the Cortez brothers the right to leave the scene. They would give their story to the police the next day. Both men walked through the crowd shaking hands with the locals. They were given a free space to allow them to approach an awaiting car. Tami stood there shaking her head while opening the door. In the car, the brother told Tami about the incident.

Tami knew what to get Cortez for Christmas. She knew he didn't like small rodents. A nephew had a hamster and Cortez wouldn't come near the cage. She figured her husband developed a phobia while young. If he was going to stay in the police business, phobias weren't allowed. The college offered classes on phobias. She found a small hamster cage built like a tower in Paris.

21   Rescue

THE AMBULANCE PEOPLE were inside with Jess and Jerome. The police let Derek through the growing throne. He raced to his wife's side, afraid of what he would find. He almost lost it seeing his pale wife's face in her stained gown. He touched her body and she felt cold. Both hostages were breathing oxygen and were ready for transport.

Jess could barely see Derek. Her eyes weren't working correct and her voice wouldn't come. She started coughing. Trying to get up from the transport cot, the emergency medic told her to stay still and not talk. Her heart and blood pressure jumped higher which caused the monitor to beep.

Derek was alarmed and quickly calmed. His bad reaction wouldn't help. He squeezed his wife's hand to let her know she should follow orders. She gave a slight squeeze back. Jess hadn't been unconscious long, but she was weak. She hadn't realized how much until she moved. She waved her hand.

Derek realized she was worried about Jerome. He told her Jerome looked like he would make it. She closed her eyes and drifted off from the shot they gave her. Derek tenderly kissed her forehead. The medics quickly got her onto the elevator.

Usually Derek was always alert at a scene. He didn't see the woman in the crowd when they came out of the building. The woman watched. Jess was transported in the first ambulance and Jerome was placed in the second one that immediately drove to the scene. People were pushed back to allow the ambulances driving clearance. Rhonda rode with the police to the hospital. She hadn't seen the person in the crowd. She was too upset to care about a suspect. Her friends were hurting. The grim expression on Derek's face told her his fear. Jess was his everything. There would be many sleepless nights until she was better.

The woman moved away and made her phone calls to shut her business down. Her expression was also grim. The police didn't know where she stored her gold or where her daughter was located. The Snake woman shifted her plans to fly to Indonesia sooner than planned. She contacted her man. There was no person answering Hamm Roe's phone. She figured the police had him in custody. Later she would realize his mistake. Her plans hadn't included killing Jess or her bodyguard. She wanted Jess to deliver her message to Derek. The message would make it after all.

Once Jess was safely tucked away in the hospital, Derek worked on removing her from Paris. A night private plane was chartered with a nurse on board. The two of them were flying back to Los Angeles. Tracking Snake woman would have to wait as well as any conversation with Hamm. Hamm would be expedited back to the states for further trial.

On the plane flying home, Derek held Jess's hand most of the way. The doctor told them she had smoke inhalation and would be better in two to three weeks. Her problems weren't as severe as Jerome.

Derek called his Captain.

"Put the lights up on the yacht now. I want Jess to see them when we arrive."

"Yes, sir. The tree also arrived. The ornaments are in the three boxes with the other box from the silver company."

"Load all of the items that she ordered. Oh, make sure we have lots of liquids and soft foods for her."

"I'll wake the chef and get rolling."

Derek disconnected from the call. Jess moaned a little and the nurse gave her another pain pill. She tried to smile at Derek. He gave her a kiss. Jess knew the smoke hadn't gotten to her. She would live. Her dress was gone, and she wore a soft flannel gown. Derek lifted the covers back over her. He squeezed her hand.

"Go back to sleep, love."

She struggled. There was something to ask him. "Home?"

"Yes, we're going home."

She fell asleep until they reached Los Angeles.

The new ambulance crew brought Jess to the yacht. She was awake when they brought her up the gang plank and into their bedroom. The crew left, and the nurse retired for four hours to a room prepared for her.

"We decorated exactly the way you requested. Welcome home, honey."

Jess saw the lights and the tree with the silken ribbon in champagne color. The pale silk peonies were attached. The silver ornaments contained some pieces of silver forks made into various shapes. Derek took the star fork design off the tree, so she could touch the piece.

"Oh, Derek."

"I know. We can talk more in the morning when you feel better."

"Okay."

Jess didn't want to let Derek know just yet that she met the Snake woman in person. The conversation would not sit well with him. He had been unable to protect her. She knew it was her fault for going after Hamm without alerting security. She didn't have any idea who the person was with Hamm until it was too late. Besides, she didn't want Derek to leave her. His revenge could wait. She was enjoying the attention.

During the night, she dreamed. There was another fire on the horizon. Jess woke up feeling sad. There would be loss.

Then, her twin daughters came bouncing in her room in the morning. Later she talked briefly with Justin and Sami on the phone. Derek and Jess walked slowly around the yacht deck.

"We'll need to postpone our annual party. The timing is not right. You need to heal. I'm sorry this happened."

Jess nodded. "July?"

"That would be a better date."

Jess needed to confess.

"Promise me . . ."

"Shh, enough talking for now. I'll promise you the world, my magical wife. But first, your health takes priority, and I can also wait for more."

Jess was glad he said magical. She also knew he would wait for her anywhere. He mentioned more. She wanted more.

Derek wrapped his arms around his precious wife. They would take things slow and easy. He had all the time in the world. His desk was handed over to Rhonda for the next month. The office shut down at Christmas for a week during their normal routine.

Normal was where the Wrights wanted to be. Healing was required from the scare of their lives. It was a gift that the two people in Paris were found in time. The Wrights would be thankful.

The other side of the world wouldn't be normal or so fortunate. A small group of terrorists were making plans to hit Indonesia. There was a diplomat on the Indonesian airplane that was the real target.

22   Interview with Hamm

THE WEATHER COOLED in Los Angeles in January. The police and officials worked fast to get Hamm Roe out of their country. They knew about Snake woman and didn't want anything to do with her possible accomplices. She had been wise to not take any hit assignments in France.

Derek walked into the room with Rhonda. Hamm looked up and slinked down in his chair. He lost weight worrying about his potential new crimes. His body was lankier.

"I don't want to talk to you. I thought they were giving me someone else. Oh, man. Can I go?"

Derek looked at a shell of a person. He was so skinny that Derek was reminded of a slinky toy. Derek grinned at the image. He was in his comfort zone interviewing the bad guy.

"Rhonda, go get Mr. Roe a cola out of the machine. I'd like a minute alone with him."

Rhonda looked skeptical.

"It's all right, isn't it, Mr. Roe?"

Hamm looked doubtful. Rhonda left the room. Derek was the man in control.

"Tell me about Snake woman."

"Who's Snake woman?"

Jess informed Derek of the entire conversations at the warehouse when she was locked away. Her help with the police produced a picture drawing of her abductor. A photo was circulating internationally of Snake woman's image to the police and airports.

"Danielle Ashley."

Hamm's mouth dropped open. His crimes were nothing compared to her crimes. His mind raced.

"I didn't know who she was. All I did was work as a forklift driver and then inspected some cream in jars. She paid me well for African standards. You can ask her foreman, Akash. He knows that is all that I did."

Derek shut the folder and got up to leave.

"Okay, okay, don't leave just yet. My lawyer explained this meeting was important. I didn't know we were going to bring Jess to a warehouse. That was totally unplanned. She drew her gun first. I just reacted and drew mine next. Perhaps Jess and her bodyguard couldn't see her move first. I didn't know what to do when she had me put them in a cell. Like I'm her employee. I must do what I'm told or else. She warned me. She would hurt Maura."

Derek said, "Who's Maura?"

"My wife. She works for a mine in Mali as a guide. Don't you see, this was not my fault. No, no. I can't be blamed for this job. I had to protect my wife first. The only way out was to run, but Danielle would find Maura. So, I thought about things. I called the fire department a good ten minutes early before I paid the vagrants to start the fire. It was so simple. Get the fire department to help because there was a bomb in the building which could blow any second and . . ."

Derek reached across the table with one hand and grabbed Hamm Roe by the neck. He started lifting the man off the chair in a strangle hold. Rhonda walked in and dropped the pop can. She grabbed Derek's hand and shouted at him to stop.

Slowly, Derek released his grip and sat down. He explained to Rhonda who started the warehouse fire.

Rhonda took control of the interview.

"You have confessed to kidnaping and starting a fire in a foreign country. It's fortunate for you that we have precedence. Once your sentence here is completed, France will want to prosecute their case. Are you clear? You need to nod your head or something if you can't speak."

Hamm wished the cola wasn't on the floor. Rhonda saw his look and picked up the can. She tilted the top away from her as she opened it. Then she walked over to the trash and poured the liquid out.

Hamm swallowed dry spit. "I don't want to go back to my old Los Angeles prison. The Green Stream people are there. They want to hurt me all the time. I need protection from them."

"Tell us something about Snake woman and we'll think about your incarceration facility."

Hamm's mind was a blank on the word incarceration. He hoped Maura would visit him in jail, but not the same day as Annabelle.

"Akash told me Danielle's plans after Paris were Indonesia with her daughter."

"Any specific place or length of time in Indonesia."

"No, nothing specific."

Derek left the room to contact his officials. The search would be focused in one country.

"Well, Hamm, it looks like you hit the bingo jackpot."

"I did?"

"We'll put you in a different prison for the rest of your term here."

"Thank you."

Rhonda left the room. She knew that she needed to hurry to catch the next plane out. She called Skid to let him know her flight plans to Jakarta.

Hamm was taken back to his holding cell.

23   Jakarta

THE PLANE LANDED on the runway and Rhonda was relieved. The flight was a long one. The officials met her at the gate with their interpreters and she was whisked away to her hotel room. She would meet with the police the next day and airport security. Rhonda let Derek and Skid know the next game plan.

If Snake woman was anywhere in the area, they hoped she would fly out of Jakarta. If they didn't catch her here, they weren't sure if they ever would. The woman could disappear for another five to ten years. Her monetary resources were endless.

Two weeks went by and there was no appearance by Snake woman.

Rhonda called Derek.

"We have nothing."

"I figured as much. I'm going to send Brandon Keller to replace you temporarily. Your calendar shows that you are supposed to be on vacation."

"Thanks, Derek. I'll contact Skid. We will probably go surfing here before the hurricane hits and then go inland."

"Wow, hurricane. I better get Brandon on a plane fast."

"Good. Is there anything new at the office?"

"One of Danielle's or Snake woman's shipments to her Paris warehouse fell and opened onto the tarmac. The cream jars broke. Guess what was in the bottom of the jar?"

"I have no idea."

"Gold spread all over the runway. The shipment came from Mali. The African officials have no clue how much gold was smuggled out of their country. Therefore, she has been put on their list of criminals. France is currently not happy about the incident. Akash and a few others were arrested in Mali. Akash implicated Hamm. He not only inspected the jars but placed gold in them. Therefore, Hamm lied to us once again. Gold smuggling has been added to Hamm Roe's crimes. There is no way that the man will make parole anywhere."

"We knew that she was into something heavy. Who would have thought Africa and France were her location? Hamm has always been a putz on my radar screen."

"I've got to ring off. The diamond necklace from the fashion show has arrived and I want to take Jess for a drive."

"Did the builder complete your casita?"

"Yes. The garage for the helicopter and two pads are also in. The basement and shell of the main structure is installed. They put in some temporary stairs to allow us a walk-through of the rooms. She will be surprised. The casita was halfway complete when Jess went to Paris. She has no idea that I started the other build plans when we flew her home. The builder brought in extra teams to get this far."

"I like the idea of the two of you building a special new place. That is so sweet."

"Oh, one more thing. Annabelle finally went to visit Hamm yesterday. I don't know what happened except Maura was there an hour ahead of her. Hamm suddenly has become ill. They took him to the infirmary. Consequently, his arraignment has been postponed two weeks."

"That's very interesting. The rat has gotten caught eating two pieces of cheese. I told you about Cortez and the manhole cover?"

"Oh, yes. That was too funny. We should get them costumes for our annual party in July."

Rhonda couldn't help but laugh. She knew the perfect costume and rental place.

"Tell Jess that we are glad she is feeling better."

"I'll do that very thing. Take care of Skid."

Derek hung up. His secretary came into his office and pointed at the psychologist report still in the in box. Derek shook his head. He would get to the report later. Grabbing his jacket, he left the office.

24   Ride with Jess

DEREK STOPPED AT the yacht. Jess was waiting for him. Their security vehicles would follow them on the ride to their new homesite. The picnic basket was prepared by their chef.

He couldn't stop looking at his beautiful wife. He had loved her for a long time. Jess was the only person that Derek truly wanted. He was glad Dean Crain helped bring Jess around. Otherwise, his life would have been lonely.

Jess smiled. Derek opened the top of the car to let some air into their space. He turned the heater on. He didn't want her feet to get cold.

"Are you warm enough?"

"I'm more than that. I feel loved and am grateful we have this day for a ride. I was feeling stuck on the yacht. My calendar is empty for three months other than the twins and you."

"I like that your calendar is empty. I won't need to schedule my time with you."

"Was it really that bad?"

Derek didn't want to talk about schedules anymore.

"Skid is flying to Jakarta to vacation with Rhonda. Brandon will take over for the duration."

"Jakarta. The place sounds interesting."

Derek drove the Los Angeles freeway in quiet silence. She knew Derek was taking her to their homesite to see if the casita was completed. When they drove through their gates, Jess was pleased. Derek had the guard house completed. There was no one there so he used the remote control. The wrought iron gates swung open. They drove the short drive to the top of the hill.

Jess gasped.

"The casita is done, the helicopter area, and the partial house. Oh, Derek, that is so sweet."

It was Derek's turn to laugh.

"Rhonda said the same thing."

Opening the car door for her, they walked to the casita first. His security people placed the picnic basket on the table and discreetly exited.

Jess went through the casita. The furniture she selected was in place. Her designer also hung the drapes and pictures. Pleasure showed in her face. The bedroom was all cream colors in varying hues. There stood a huge basket of flowers in the room and a silver vase of chilled champagne. A large decanter of flavored water was on the table with ice in case Jess wasn't ready for the alcohol.

"It's beautiful, Derek. Our guests will like the space."

"Heck, I like the space. I thought we could give the casita a whirl if you are ready?"

Jess looked at her sweet husband.

"I'm ready except we need to explore first."

"Okay. Let's do the tour."

They walked around the helicopter garage and he showed her how they easily could roll the helicopter into each stall electronically or manually.

153

They walked around the two helicopter pads. She noted the trees were removed from the property to allow the required clearance. Moving to the main structure, Derek explained the location of each room. Jess remembered the architect's drawing.

"You have moved the pool twenty or thirty feet to the left."

"We did the move to allow space for the bar and barbeque area. There will be a partial roof for the area where we have placed tables. On the other end of the pool, the architect was wanting to put a berm or hill. Then outsiders can't see our pool."

"Why don't we put in pavers, more tables, and a second barbeque/bar area. That way, we can have an hors d'oeuvre location and a main meal station. The berm could be pushed out further and we could install a brick plant structure to provide additional screening. It might be fun to put in a sandpit with a top for a children's play area. Even a little wading pool. Someday we may have grandchildren."

"And you are going to want more potted plants around this new area?"

Jess hugged her husband.

"Yes, please."

"Are you ready for lunch?"

Derek had a twinkle in his eye.

"Very ready."

They walked back to the casita hand in hand. Their afternoon lunch was more than sweet.

25   Annabelle's Plan

THE REALIZATION THAT Hamm Roe had not only been unfaithful but remarried was a crime. He was married to someone else while still married to her rankled more than the feathers in Annabelle's roost. She looked at her cheap wedding ring. She married Hamm while he was in jail. She waited for him. Then his escape was a miracle. She was a real wife for months. Hamm robbed her of her pride and dignity.

The disaster of a husband was too much for Annabelle. Plus, the Maura person was prettier than Annabelle. One day Annabelle looked up the meaning of Maura and it read *star of the sea*. Her name meant *joy*. She didn't feel joyful. Hamm crossed the sea to find a new star wife. The idea rankled. Her mind went around and around those facts.

Annabelle would run into the woman at the prison. Payback was the only record playing over and over in her brain. She wished her brother was still alive. Now Annabelle would need to be strong. She made her decision. Hamm must pay.

There was no way to get the Green Stream Nevada people inside the prison where the police would eventually take Hamm. Annabelle couldn't ask her cousin, Randy Moore, for help because he was a straight arrow ever since he opened his first restaurant. She couldn't ask Brake or Caro, her biker friends, because Brake would tell Randy. She thought about Amy, and she couldn't use her. Her brother, Minnow

Surf tried to kill Amy. Therefore, Annabelle was at a loss for any friend's help.

Her doorbell rang and there stood Randy Moore's wife, Sandra. Annabelle didn't want to deal with her today but knew she should be polite. She invited Sandra into the living room. Her house had rooms separate from each other. No one would see the mess in the kitchen, bathrooms, or bedrooms.

"Annabelle, sweetheart, we are so worried about you. Randy suggested that I come visit. Amy would have come but we're not sure how you feel about the loss of your brother, Minnow."

"Oh, I'm okay with Amy. Minnow didn't redo his prescription nor read the krispy bar labels. That was not Amy's fault. He knew about the risk from a peanut allergy. I would have picked up his medicine except he didn't ask. How was I to know that he needed my help? Do you still carry your gun in your purse?"

Sandra said, "Good." She stopped and looked at Annabelle.

"Now, Annabelle, you just forget about my gun. There's no reason for you to jump off the deep end. Let him stew in his own mess. Our conversation makes my suggestion easier. We know your husband, Hamm Roe, is going to trial for new crimes. We feel for you. Amy has offered her beauty shop services for a cut, color, blow-dry, and new style. She wants you to look pretty. A woman feels better after the beauty shop. I can drive you to the beauty shop which is close to us and include the nail job. What do you think about that? Then, Randy has offered a new outfit into the mix. I'll send over several ones you can choose from. Plus, there's super-pretty and shapely flat shoes on the market. They have rhinestones on top. A little sparkle never hurt anyone. I'll include some of those and sweet body-fitting purses. Red is good or tan. I'll include both and you can choose your outfit. I know women like to select their own stuff. What do you say? Let's give you a new killer-look for the court appearance."

Annabelle wasn't listening until Sandra mentioned something that drew her attention.

"I guess your suggestions will be just the ticket. I usually wear tan. Red sounds better. Yes, let's do red. Red screams killer. Can I have one of those new necklaces with lots of stones? Maybe pearls, too. Pearls would look good on me."

Sandra said, "That's the spirit. We knew you needed our love and support at this disastrous time. I know the greatest place. One of my friends at the beauty shop sells jewelry out of her home. I'll get her to send you pictures. You decide. I want you to select the best one because you are worth every penny, my friend. You get the necklace that is a statement piece. Let that necklace shout, *go girl!*"

Randy Moore's wife was never one to sit by the sidelines. She supported women in their fight for equality. Her viewpoint of Hamm was dirt bag and let's dump him in the Mariana Trench. Jail-hell was too good a place.

Annabelle jumped up enthusiastically. She wanted to look like a million bucks at the court appearance. She would look like a star.

"Let fashion begin!"

Sandra was so surprised by Annabelle's over-enthusiasm. All she could do was hug the woman and leave. Randy would be pleased with her success. Everything was arranged for Annabelle's transformation.

There was only one way out of this mess. Divorce hadn't even occurred to Annabelle. However, with Sandra and Randy Moore's help, she was going to look perfect as a first wife. She would look the part- -a beautiful, attentive wife who was attending her husband's trial. The new look would throw Hamm into a tizzy. He would regret his error in judgment in more ways than one.

She contacted a few members of the Nevada gang that weren't in jail. Annabelle knew one of the Nevada gang who owed her a favor. She always knew the favor still stood open. Minnow still owned lingering friends in the business. The trick was, *how not to get caught*!

She went back to the jail to visit Hamm one last time and found out her husband was in the infirmary. All Annabelle had to do was wait and see if Hamm died. She hoped this solution would work or else the other plan would be implemented. Her other thought was another source. Hamm told her about Derek Wright choking him when he found out Hamm started the fire where Jess was held. Annabelle hoped

Derek would do the choking thing at the courthouse. She knew this last plan was wishful thinking.

The Nevada friend went online to see which cases were going to appear on the docket. The first week, there was nothing. The second week, there still was not the correct name. The third week was the same. Finally, the fourth week, the name Hamm Roe appeared.

The cleaning crew was arranged for the date Hamm Roe was on the schedule. The gun was planted along with several other guns. The game would be confusion at the height of creativity. A switch of instruments and players would leave the police on a goose chase. The Nevada group was confident as they used this same plan once before in robbing a small bank.

Annabelle looked at herself in the mirror. She was smiling too much. Those types of smiles would be a dead giveaway. She got the giggles. That piece of action wouldn't work. She tried her blank look. Annabelle felt this look nailed perfectly her disguise. She walked around her apartment practicing.

She was pleased to carry a secret. Hamm wouldn't know what struck him. She saw images of a volcano on a television show. The molten yellow fire intrigued Annabelle.

26   Annabelle's Justice

IF BAD EVENTS were happening, a courthouse was more than likely not a good place to implement them. The reason for this was the unusual number of security people, police, prosecutors, etc. that roamed the building during the day. The Nevada group were lucky. Hamm Roe was the last person on the docket. Most of the above people would have left the building and security would be lighter.

The Nevada group waited until the arraignment was over. This was the normal time for the cleaning crew to arrive. They highjacked the cleaning truck, depositing the original cleaning crew at a local sandpit, tied to a grader. A little duct tape helped to secure them under the grader's frame. A message would be given to the judge the next day about their whereabouts. The Nevada group couldn't kill the real cleaning crew because they weren't the target.

Maura took her seat in the courtroom and looked at Annabelle in disdain when she entered the room. Annabelle walked to the front of the court room like she was a model on a runway. Annabelle put her nose in the air and sat down in an aisle seat. She wasn't anybody's fool. She could play snooty.

Derek decided not to appear at the arraignment for fear that he would kill Hamm Roe. He was still pissed at the man's stupidity in placing Jess in harm's way. He sent his retired detective friend, Jim Michaels, to watch the show.

Jim noticed the two women. He said to himself, *hell hath no fury*. Then he saw Hamm Roe enter the courtroom. His shackles rose. Jim would have liked to strangle the man himself or used his gun. The gun would be faster. It was too bad; the special metal item was in his trunk. However, Jim wouldn't risk the consequences of either weapon. He learned a long time ago how to master emotion. Fortunately, Hamm owned no money and couldn't make bail. The amount would have been astronomical if the court's allowed bail. Jim forgot to ask Derek about bail and figured the item was the least of his worries today. He brought a book along on fishing in case things were boring.

Jim frowned. Annabelle looked a little strange. She seemed wooden. He was reminded of a voodoo doll. Her blush was blotchy. The other woman, Maura, was impeccably dressed, wearing a black suit, and sitting on the edge of her seat like a frightened rabbit. Jim dismissed his thoughts about the women. He wondered if something was going down. Maybe he should have brought his wife, Mary Beth with him. She was better at assessing a woman's true nature.

The courtroom seemed hot and stuffy from too many cases shoved through the system in one day. The smell of sweat permeated the room. Looking at Hamm Roe in a white shirt, he could tell the man was sweating. Hamm tripped on his foot guard. He glanced at Annabelle in screaming red. Next, he looked at her bright yellow flats with red crystals. She looked like a volcano about to erupt. He thought to himself, "What happened to her?"

Next, he searched the courtroom for his second wife, Maura. Maura half stood. Hamm smiled at his second wife. As Hamm sat down, Jim noticed how red Annabelle's face became. There must be some anger there were Jim's thoughts.

The judge ruffled the pages, looked at the suspect, the two wives, the attorneys, and read the charges. Hamm pled not guilty. The judge looked at Hamm's attorney with raised eyebrows. The attorney shrugged and nodded. The judge shrugged his shoulders back and didn't alter the bail amount. A future date was set for the preliminary hearing. The accused rose to return to his jail cell. The judge had risen and stopped to talk with the bailiff. The attorneys were packing their briefcases.

Jim couldn't believe Hamm was trying the not guilty route. The evidence would prove otherwise. The man was a nit-wit. Jim quickly exited the courtroom with his book and took the stairs out of the building.

Upon hearing a single gunshot fire, Jim ran back in the building and paused on the stair for breath. A cleaning crew came racing past him and out the door. Jim paid them no mind and continued to the top of the stairs. He almost ran into the security people who pushed him aside. Jim continued up the stairs and back to the courtroom where a woman was screaming.

"My nightmare, my nightmare. No, no, no. This can't be happening. Not Hamm. Help him. Somebody, you must help him."

Jim saw Maura as the female screaming and she slipped to the floor crying. Annabelle was still sitting in the courtroom with a blank expression on her face. She hadn't moved one inch and showed no emotion. He wondered if Annabelle was in shock.

Jim looked around the room. His eyes stopped at the glass door where guards took out the prisoners. The glass part of the door had blood splatter and there was Hamm Roe's face screwed up in a painful expression. He looked like a mad man. His white shirt contained a spreading red blob. Water from a bucket soaked his shirt blurring the body image. A metal cart was behind the wounded criminal. The mops and brooms were holding the body upright. The man's eyes weren't blinking anymore. Jim knew the man was dead.

The guards were ushering the judge out the opposite door. Most of the people in the courtroom were crouched under their seats. It was an odd scene when the police arrived and let the people in the room go. Jim watched Annabelle leave. He thought he saw a smirk on her face.

Jim exited the building after talking with the police and watching the ambulance remove the victim. He entered his vehicle and contacted Derek.

The police didn't catch the shooters or find a gun around the courtroom. Jim and Derek wondered how the gang pulled this one off. They weren't exactly sure which gang did the deed and didn't exactly pursue any investigation. Derek said there was no use wasting money on a dead bloke. Jim agreed, only bloke was too kind a word. Jim would let his friend in Napa hear about the strange courtroom murder. Officer Simms from Napa, California, would be pleased another dirt bag lost.

Stew Avery or Hamm Roe, a minor con artist, was conned out of prison and his life. The only person that missed him was a second wife. Even the second wife's grief was suspect. She was seen shopping the next day at a new hotel.

Annabelle was working out at a new gym that sponsored private yoga classes. Sandra helped her select new leotards and tops. Then Sandra showed her coffee shops where she could meet potential friends. The Moore's bought her a thousand-dollar gift card at the coffee shop. Annabelle was checking out the new scene. There were other people besides her reeling from grief. Annabelle made friends and joined a knitting class to expand her horizon.

27   Jakarta Airport

RHONDA AND SKID took longer than a two-week vacation. A bridge to their resort was washed out and the small landing strip was blocked with trees. It took two more weeks to get a helicopter to fly them to the airport. They were flying to Sydney, Australia and onto Los Angeles. Brandon would stay two more weeks and then all of Derek's crew would be back in the states.

Rhonda and Skid were sitting at their gate. Their plane was delayed another hour due to a mechanical issue. Skid was a little nervous about the mechanical problem and hoped this airline used new parts instead of recycled ones. Rhonda assured him their airline was one of the better ones. She checked out their safety record.

"Watch my roller bag, Skid, I have to use the ladies room. I'll stroll to the one on the end of the terminal. The two restrooms look the same distance."

"All right. Grab me a bottle of orange juice on your way back."

Rhonda came out of the ladies' room and looked below at the smaller plane loading passengers. The plane was boarding, and the passengers walked the tarmac to the movable steps. People disappeared inside the doorway of the airliner. A few stragglers were running to get on the plane. Rhonda turned to see if there was a line at the juice place. There wasn't one. She moved to go and stopped.

A woman was pushing a wheelchair with another female rider holding a leather backpack. The backpack looked designer quality. The two people were wearing the same black colored outfits. The only difference was the color of their thin stockings. One had black nylons and the other wore white. The two females appeared to look alike. It was hard to tell from the angle where she was standing. The woman pushing the chair looked directly at Rhonda and quickly continued to the steps of the plane.

Rhonda walked to the juice bar and brought Skid his bottle.

"Thanks. You took a long time getting my juice."

"I did. There was a plane, and I watched as the passengers stepped across the tarmac. I believe the gate sign read Flight 1498 for Hong Kong."

"Did you see anything interesting?"

Rhonda put her head on Skid's shoulder.

"I'm so tired that my eyes hurt."

"Aw, let me kiss them better."

Rhonda looked at the gate down the long corridor. The area appeared empty. Rhonda started fidgeting, getting up from her seat, and sitting down again. The loudspeaker blared that their plane would board in thirty minutes.

"What's the matter Rhonda? You're biting your lip."

"I think that I saw her down at the other gate. She was with someone."

"Which gate?"

"I didn't catch the number. It was the Hong Kong flight."

Skid said, "Gate 35."

"Oh, no. We have to stop that plane." She grabbed her phone, talking fast to Brandon, while running toward the end of the terminal. Skid was trying to catch up with their luggage in tow.

"It's gone."

"I see there is no airplane here."

Rhonda tried redialing Brandon and her cell phone died.

"Give me your phone quick."

Skid dropped the handles of their rollaway bags and fished in the zipper side pocket.

"Here you go."

Brandon answered, "Hello, Skid."

"No, it's Rhonda. Did they stop the Flight 1498?"

"She's airborne. We're too late."

"Have the control tower contact the pilot and have the police notified to pick up the two women when they deplane in Hong Kong." Rhonda described their approximate height, hair color, clothes, and wheelchair.

Rhonda collapsed in her chair. She was still on her phone.

"I hope that I'm right. We should see if there are any tapes from the outside camera. We need a copy for Derek."

Brandon said, "I'll talk with security."

Skid collected their luggage.

"I think we missed our flight. We need to go to our gate and see."

The two weary travelers went back to their gate. Rhonda approached the steward. He motioned for them to wait. The steward was talking to the gate person. Another plane was returning to a designated gate. All the passengers were directed to a different gate for a newer airplane.

Rhonda and Skid moved fast to get an upgrade to their tickets at the next gate. Skid was working the phone while Rhonda flagged down a cart vehicle. They were going to fly back to the states in style. They left Brandon to handle the mess of catching Snake woman and contact Derek.

28   Flight 1498 Missing

AS SOON AS Rhonda and Skid landed in LA, Derek called her.

"Talk to me, Rhonda. Exactly what did you see at the airport in Jakarta."

Rhonda described the episode to him while Skid retrieved their vehicle.

"I've got to hang up. Brandon is on my other line. I'll get back to you."

"Brandon, here. We can't get a copy of the tape outside Gate 35. The whole airport is in turmoil and security doesn't have time to deal with our problem. The flight to Hong Kong is missing. The plane never landed. They have search planes out now looking for debris. No one knows what went wrong."

Derek said, "Are you thinking storm or mechanical failure? Was there any distress call? They must know some information."

"Right now, communication about the airplane is in lockdown mode. I hope there weren't terrorists involved. The government heard a few rumors but thought there was a smoke screen put up to make people nervous."

"Why would they pick Indonesia?"

Brandon was rubbing his hand. "Who knows? We just need to figure out if Snake woman was on the airplane and who was with her? We can use Jess's photo drawing to compare the taped video of the two women boarding the airplane. That's why the tape is our ticket to enlightenment."

"Where are the family members of the passengers?"

"The potential family members are being sent to a separate lounge in the airport. I'll see if they will allow me to talk with the families. Some of these people may have talked with the two women. It's worth a shot."

"Yes, Brandon, go to the lounge. Do you want Rhonda to fly back there?"

"No, you need her in LA. There are the cases we exchanged that need her attention."

Derek called Rhonda back on her cell and updated her. He let her know Brandon was staying in Jakarta until their office was satisfied with the information.

Skid came to a screeching halt in their vehicle to pick Rhonda up. He helped her with the luggage and they drove to Ara and Jack Jones place to pick up Skid's daughter, Maggie.

Once Maggie was settled in bed, Rhonda poured a glass of iced tea for herself and Skid.

"Why the worried look?"

"I'm thinking of all those passengers. The airplane probably has a hundred on board. Then there's the two women. What if the other person is someone important? Her backpack is current fashion for the younger set. There was an owl leather tag on the zipper and lots of grommets."

"Are you thinking a celebrity for the backpack person?"

"No, I'm thinking a daughter."

"Snake woman's daughter? That would be a disaster," said Skid.

"Exactly."

They turned on the evening news and watched the announcement regarding the missing airliner. No one claimed responsibility for the failure. Airplane's don't just fall from the sky. The airport was a mess of people with anxious looks on their faces. Photographers and news people were descending upon the area. Rhonda knew that it would be some time before they could see the video tapes of the gate. In the meantime, everyone would have to sit tight.

Two days later, the officials found the wide swath of floating debris. The news media somehow obtained a video of the ocean where they believed the plane dumped. Derek knew there was a bomb on board. Terrorists brought the airplane down. He wondered which cell would count the mess as their victory. The leader of that group would become the hunted or already was on the long list of known players. Derek didn't know what the airport tapes would reveal. The game would step to a higher level. There would be no place the leader of the terrorist group could hide.

Jess knew the sadness she felt earlier was her inner thoughts sending a warning. Derek told her about the two women. She thought, like Rhonda, there existed the possibility of the daughter being on the plane. There were mothers and daughters who looked alike. She could believe this possibility existed between Snake woman and her daughter.

29   Boarding Video

THE BOARDING VIDEO arrived at Derek's office. Rhonda and Brandon were in Derek's conference room. Brandon had previewed the tape in Jakarta. He was anxious to get his partners' opinions.

They reviewed the boarding scene. The picture Rhonda portrayed to Derek earlier came alive on the large television screen. Derek zoomed in the frame of the two women. A younger version of Snake woman sat in the wheelchair with white nylon stockings. They stopped at the bottom of the steps to the airplane.

Another couple with large suitcases blocked the two women for a moment. The steward came down the steps to see what the problem was with the suitcases. They were too large for the overhead bin. The steward contacted a baggage person with her remote. The baggage person now blocked the view of the couple. Two men pushed passed the entourage and rushed up the steps.

Derek stopped the tape.

"Now those two men look highly suspicious. They only have briefcases."

Brandon said, "Oops, I usually stuff underwear and a shirt in a briefcase. I hate to carry a bag on the plane. The upper bins are always full."

"Let's ask the police to run their faces as well as the two women."

Derek hit the button to resume the video. The couple went up the steps, moving slowly like their feet hurt. The two women remained at the bottom of the plane. The one in the wheelchair stood up and walked over to the other woman. She hugged the other woman and ran up the steps of the plane. Derek and Rhonda were surprised. The wheelchair was a disguise. The attendant came and took the wheelchair away.

The woman with the black nylons turned and walked away from the airplane. She disappeared back into the terminal building. They saw she held a ticket in her hand. The flight data wasn't visible.

The flight attendant on the airliner shut the door. The steps were moved away, and the Indonesian plane was pushed away from the gate. The airliner turned to taxi to the runway. The video ended.

It occurred to Rhonda and Derrick that the woman escaped on some other airplane. There were many other smaller planes that flew to the other islands around Jakarta. The planes were small charter companies.

Brandon told them there was a second video of when the woman walked through the door, back inside the terminal. The second video loaded.

"Rhonda said, "Hold it, back up the second video."

Derek said, "She looks like any of a hundred women at an airport. There's nothing unusual."

"Don't you see it? Her roller bag is on the right and she used her left hand to retrieve her bag."

Derek watched the video again.

"Are you thinking she is lefthanded?"

"I'm thinking exactly that. She may be one of ten percent of the people in the world who are lefthanded."

Brandon piped up, "Or she could be ambidextrous."

"Yes, but unconsciously, she will use her left hand."

Derek turned off the video.

"I don't believe it. She didn't get on Flight 1498. I wonder why she didn't travel with the other woman to Hong Kong? Who do the women know in Hong Kong? Well, we have confirmation that Snake woman is alive. Brandon, did you contact the charter companies?"

"Yes, the list is a long one of companies."

Rhonda jumped up from her chair.

"I'll help with the list."

They left Derek alone. He replayed the tapes and stopped the image on the wheelchair. He saw the owl tag with fuzzy fur around the eyes. He knew who she was.

"The daughter."

Derek ejected the video, made a copy, and walked out to his secretary. She placed the original in the awaiting envelope for the police and took the small USB stick for placement in their files.

He didn't know what other course of action they could take. He was stunned at the turn of events. Derek wondered which evil person she would take out first. Revenge would be her motive. Murder would be her solution. Money wouldn't matter. Men or whoever was responsible would die. The reason they would die was her only solution for bad people.

His secretary knocked and entered his office. Derek was making a new batch of coffee.

"Here, let me do that for you. Take this folder. The terrorist group is known. There was an announcement. They are a small band in Syria, elusive, and hard to find."

Derek read the name of the leader and perused the other names that belonged to this group. Two of the men on the airport tape would match exactly the images of two men on the terrorist list. Snake woman's video image would be a 90 percent match to Jess's drawing.

"Where will you strike—Mali or Syria? Both countries will be a challenge for your entrance and exit but then, Houdini girl, go for it. I do believe we are sitting the next few months out of the game. I will stop tracking you for a while. You can take care of your family's business. Jess and I have a party to plan and attend."

Derek looked at the psychologist report still in his in box. His secretary placed several dated yellow sticky notes on top.

"Please read." "Please read now." "I give up." Derek smiled. He threw the notes away and placed the report in his briefcase. Perhaps he could find some time to finish reading the darn report. At least his secretary would be happy.

"Lefthanded, now that's something new. It's certainly worth noting in her file."

30 Annual Party

JULY WAS AS good a time as any to have a party in San Francisco. Jess was able to rent an entire pier for the evening. The stage would be long and thin to accommodate the movement of the musician acts. The players were as follows: Justin Wright, son and young rock star; Wade Brookston, Rhonda's friend and aged rock star. Included in the performances were race car driver/singer, Mic Palla. Palla's friends, Terrelle Triumphs, were also part of the performer list. The Cortez brothers were doing a skit about a cat, bad guy, and rats in an alley. Their costumes, of course, were the rats. The bad guy was plastic surgeon, Jack Jones, Ara's husband. He wanted to try his hand at being stupid. Dan Jaehn, another race car driver, and Mic would hand out autographs and black stuffed panthers to the children.

The food would be vendor trucks brought on site and at the end of the street near the beer tent. Every kind of fish imaginable would be on the menu. A gourmet salad vendor was chosen for the cold salads. A special vendor for the children was also brought in. Carmel apples with chocolate would be a hit. Kabobs of fruit, fried cheese, and chicken were included. The chicken was compressed into snake shapes. It was something Jess chose at the last minute. She believed Derek wouldn't mind. There were tiny donuts with three kinds of flavored sugar. Suckers were small blueberry stars and vanilla moons.

The dress theme was anything from the 50's through the 90's. Optional were costumes of a person's favorite rock star.

The pearl diver store would be kept open as a diversion for the crony wives. Little did Jess know, their twins, Cata and Alina would get fifteen necklaces each from the women.

The Wrights didn't have to pay for fireworks this year. The display would be put on by the city. The twinkle lights were already part of the pier décor. What Jess didn't know was that Derek paid a lighting company to add twinkle lights all around their new house pool area.

There would be no drones this year due to new laws. A balloon company would drop fresh sardines to keep the sea otters out of the area for a little while and entertain the children who watched the catch, release, and catch again play of the creatures before they ate.

Their warehouse in San Francisco would be the drop-off location for the vehicles, and special buses would run their guests back and forth. One side of the roadway was blocked off for the buses.

When the other pier owners heard wind of the party, they offered the Wrights a deal. All extra proceeds from their vendors would belong to the Wrights, and they could have full use of their pier. Consequently, three piers in a row were designated for the party.

Large jumbo-Tron television screens were installed so everyone could watch the spectacular performances. Special lighting was placed to illuminate the stage. There was no room for plants or decorations which made the party less work for Jess.

Special buoys were used to keep boats away from the piers. The police protection and presence would be heavy with the Napa department invited along with the city's police. Invitations were special first name badges encoded for the day to allow people to move between the piers.

✗✗✗✗✗✗

Derek and Jess were exhausted as their limousine drove away from the pier. They and their family were allowed the luxury of limousines.

"Wow, that was a great time. I have never talked or laughed so much. Thank you for the party. Dean would have been proud, especially the skit. The Cortez brothers played out the capture of Hamm to perfection."

"Yes, it was hilarious. Justin, Wade, Mic and the Terrelle's singing dual was funny, too. I'm glad everyone had a good time. Our people know the party closes at midnight. I'm sure they will still be there, especially the San Francisco group. They kept talking to me about Dean. I have another collection of stories to tell you. And they took my Paris bodyguard, Jerome, under their wing for the duration of his weekend stay."

"Great. Did you see Harry Jenkins and his wife made it to our party? He was hobnobbing with the San Francisco police about a case they were working. It

180

was good to talk with him. He told me that the FBI set up an interview when he gets back."

"It would be good business to have a close friend there."

Derek slid closer to Jess. "I do think we have a problem for next year."

"Why is there a problem?" Jess squeezed his hand. She knew there was no problem because her husband was smiling.

"The crony wives cornered me along with Tami, Tiare, and Rhonda. They want next year's annual party to be at our new house. They offered to help with the planning and offered their husband's wallets to pay any extras. I told them we would think about their generous offer. Rhonda offered to helicopter people to our site if the drive got too full."

"Oh, my. Isn't our group a little crazy. Will there be room?"

"A little crazy? I have a sneaky feeling where they get the way-overboard syndrome. More like nuts is my thought. As far as room, we can try to expand some more."

Jess punched him in the arm for the reference to nuts and laughed. The limousine arrived at the private jet waiting to take them back to Los Angeles. Derek and Jess were spending the night in their new home. Their children were staying in San Francisco in hotels with Skid and Rhonda, Jim and his wife, and the Cortez/Miami group.

When they reached their house, Derek brought out the old bottle of scotch. He poured Jess half a glass and filled the rest with water.

"Toast? I wanted to wait until we were alone. The fireworks were nice. I was impressed by the city's display."

"The lights here around the pool are wonderful. You are my sweet husband. Absolutely, a toast to us and Dean Crain. Although he is gone, we still miss him. He would be pleased how our family has held together. Life is very good."

Jess walked out to the far end of their pool and looked at the city lights.

"Isn't the skyline beautiful? It's too bad we can't see the one hundred billion stars."

"I love this view. It is the best on our property. When did the stars come into the night? I see a few bright ones."

Jess shook her head. Derek knew he was missing something important. He decided to play the game.

"Only one hundred billion? That's not even close to the number I'm thinking."

He had engaged her curiosity.

"What is the number you are thinking?"

Derek knew his answer was vital to tonight.

"Let's say one galaxy is that number times five hundred galaxies."

Jess said, "Only five hundred?"

Derek laughed. "You know the number is way more."

"I love the number you are thinking. We are on the same page, and I'm in the mood to try to match the heavens."

Derek was half listening. He saw images of Dean until she said mood and match the heavens with stars.

"What kind of mood are you in?"

"Oh, Derek, the mood is of the night, whatever we make of it. Stars, heavens, everything within our reach and then some."

Jess held out her hand. Derek took his wife's hand and led her to their special place. Their romantic feelings of earthly and heavenly bodies resonated in the air.

She stopped and went hysterical when she saw the sign. It read, *Third Bedroom,* and was a diamond shape. The sign represented their own private place. It was onboard Dean's sailboat. Their first journey to find her mother's heirloom necklace was another place and a scary, beautiful time. Twin poisoners brought them together in a fight for Jess's freedom and life.

She looked at her husband and didn't want to spoil the mood. He understood.

"It's a trillion, zillion, quad-zillion, super-whatever. I'll ask our accountant tomorrow."

Derek picked her up and carried his wife over the threshold. He didn't want to discuss stars. Their new house was another beginning. The sign only a linkage to their past world.

Holding his wife in his strong arms was where she was meant to be. Jess cuddled in closer, safe and warm. There was no way Derek was going to let go.

31 Mali

AKASH WAITED AT his brother's house. His brother took out a loan and paid for Akash's bail except he wore a monitor on his leg. His lawyer argued with the courts that Akash did not benefit from his employer's gold smuggling scheme and was not a flight risk. However, he couldn't leave the house. He had tried. The porch was as far as he could go.

Akash wasn't exactly truthful. The last shipment to Paris contained two boxes. The shipment with gold was supposed to have been ten boxes. He secretly stashed the other eight boxes under his brother's porch. Flowers were planted to disguise them. Everyday Akash watered the plants with a hose from the porch. He poured a little fertilizer on the plants, so they would grow larger.

Little did he know a woman watched him from across the street. She wondered about the plants. She knew her last gold shipment was off. She read the police article in the Paris paper.

The house across the street was a place she purchased awhile back. The place was run down and didn't have a working water system. He wondered who would want such a place.

One day, Akash saw the old woman. He was not impressed. Her hair was a straggly, kinky gray. Her body was stooped over beyond all repair. He thought she probably developed rickets as a child and dismissed her as no one important. The outside of the house wasn't repaired. Her weeds were unsightly.

The old woman waited. She was very good at patience when she wanted. She called someone to deliver water once a week in large bottles. This gave her an opportunity to stand at the end of her lot while the young man switched the heavy bottles. She would glance across the street and try to see into the house. She was watchful around the dog.

The police came and took Akash away for his preliminary court hearing. They would bring him back in the evening. The old woman carried a bag of burnt cookies and left them on the porch. She peeked underneath the porch and pulled out a box. The side label and markings were from her company. She counted the boxes. All eight of the gold shipment was under the brother's porch.

The old woman put a dog treat under the wicker couch. She walked quickly across the street and made her phone calls. It was time.

The next morning, Akash made himself breakfast, fed the dog, and went to sit on the dilapidated porch with his coffee. The wicker couch creaked. His dog disappeared under the couch. The weedy flowers were three feet high now. He saw the burned cookies and looked across the street. Akash got up to throw them out back in the trash near the garage.

A truck pulled up filled with lumber and plants. A second truck appeared with workers. The foreman and a few of the men disappeared around the house. The dog barked and then was silent. The foreman gave the dog more treats. The second crew began tearing the porch down. Bins were used to collect the debris and were loaded onto the truck. A third bin was used for the scraggly plants and loaded on the second truck. When the new porch and plants were installed, the trucks drove away.

The neighbors were surprised about the new porch. The policemen watching the house didn't think anything was amiss with the new construction.

The old woman sauntered down the block with her handmade grocery bag. This was the day she went to the small market down the street. The police ignored her because they were familiar with her trips. Turning the corner, the old woman got into a beater car with her friend, Brita. The car slowly pulled away from the dirt curbing.

The brother came home and found the new porch and his brother, Akash missing. He found the dog in the house sleeping. The police ankle brace was tied around the dog's collar. The brother didn't tell the police watching his house because he assumed Akash escaped. The police wouldn't find out about the man's disappearance until the next court date.

XXXXXX

Akash awoke in a mine hole. He tried to move except he couldn't. His arms and legs were tied to a chair. Looking around, he saw a blanket, a six pack of water, and a basket of canned goods. Suddenly, a woman climbed down the stairs into the mine hole. Akash felt true fear.

"Hello, Akash. It was easy to find you. You should have run from the police. What amazes me is the fact they didn't check under your brother's house. They made a real mess of my offices and plant."

"I'm sorry."

"Yes, I see that sorry look on your face now that you are caught."

Akash didn't say anything. He was at a loss for words. She could snuff his life out at any moment. He wondered if he should pray.

"You should be afraid of me. I'm sure the police have told you who I am."

"They did mention some poisonings and murder."

"Shoot, is that all they mentioned? There is so much more."

"I don't want to die today."

"Then you should have thought of this before you stole from me."

"I was going to give it back."

"Of course, you were. However, I have seen your brother and his family. They live in a poor area. It might be nice if they could live comfortably and not have to worry about a strange woman in their future. Is the message clear regarding their future?"

"Yes, I understand completely. What do you want me to do?"

"I'll let you know. We'll leave you now to your own devices. I'm sure you know how to get out of a mine hole. There are instructions in the bag. Follow them completely."

His boss climbed up the ladder. The ladder vanished, and he was left alone. Akash looked at the soil and knew what part of the area he was buried in. The location was far from town and the current local diggings. There was no one around. The sweat poured down his face. He wasn't sure about still being alive. Deadman walking was more like it.

32   Terrorist Camp

THE WOMAN WAS brought to their camp and her weapons removed. The second man in command approached her. He bent to take the gold necklace off her neck. She kneed him in the groin and landed a karate chop to his neck. The man went down. The other terrorists drew their guns. The leader walked around the woman while his man laid in the dirt grunting.

"My man told me that you want to join our cause. This means that you will need to kill upon command. Do you have more skills that what this demonstration provided me?"

"Let me have my guns and knife. I will show you."

"You must think me a fool. If I give you the weapons, how do I know you won't use them against me."

"I have no desire to hurt you; but let's be clear, if you did something to dishonor or disfavor me, then you should run for your life."

"Ha, ha! You are not my judge and jury. We only run so we can fight tomorrow. All right. You can go with the man in the dirt on their next mission. We sleep outside with no fire. An extra blanket is all you will be provided and a canteen of water. We eat when we can steal food. Don't lose the canteen or blanket."

"Will I be told where this mission takes place and when?"

"No, you won't know until five seconds before we strike."

"Five seconds. Isn't that a little short?"

"The time is enough. Don't question me again. You will follow my procedures."

The woman looked at the other men. She memorized their names and faces. Stealing and killing were easy tasks. Waiting to kill the leader last would be extremely difficult. This effort would take all her willpower.

"Yes, sir."

Snake woman took her wool blanket and went to bed. She touched the vial in a secret pocket. The bottle was special-sealed. There was a moment of pleasure knowing the men hadn't found the snake juice. She hoped her accomplice and his men were setting the explosives and traps. Those devices were for the lesser men in the terrorist group. The money she paid for the helpers to provide services was high. She heard they were the best to flush out this group's location. Dangerous missions always cost more.

The next day, they moved to a small town and set up their strike zone. Five men from the terrorist group were with her. The men were in front of her when they stopped their forward movement. The second in command motioned for them to remain in place. There was a sound in the distance. It sounded like a truck.

The men and Snake woman moved off the road. The truck drove by. Snake woman smiled. She hung to the back of the pack as they continued walking on the road. The road did a switchback of curves. There would be another deep bend in the road with a tipped over jeep close to an old building. The ambush worked perfectly. Snake woman walked back to the terrorist camp slightly wounded. The five men didn't make the return trip.

Upon arrival, she explained to the leader what happened. He was not too happy that a new person survived. The group went back to the ambush place to bury their dead.

"Show me how you managed to escape in the dark without much blood being shed."

All the men surrounded her. Their disposition was one of disapproval and anger. She should have been afraid. There was no fear in her eyes.

Snake woman used her gun as a lever to forward flip to the top of the low building roof. She was thankful the height was only eight feet. Ten feet was a normal feat by her. Ten feet would have produced some sound. Her body gracefully and soundlessly hit the roof. The gun was slung over her left shoulder. She slid to the other side of the roof, dropped to the ground, and walked around to the men. There was no noise. Her arrival behind the men made them jump when she spoke. The men were speechless.

"All right. You move and jump like the silent jaguar. I can see how you might have escaped but I still don't trust you."

The leader knew his men walking in their heavy boots made the sound of a hundred elephants. They would have made much more noise landing on the roof. The grunts trying to do a flip would have alerted his enemies for miles. He wondered if she could do a flip backward. The leader snarled at his group to watch her until the woman gained his trust back. He remembered her brave comment about giving her a reason to kill him. Distrust versus continuance weaved around his mind. For now, they would let her continue to be a part of their group.

The woman waited until nightfall and slipped the antibiotic into her mouth. She couldn't afford to get ill. A pillowcase was stolen from the last town which she ripped into bandages.

The next two weeks were more explosives, blowing empty buildings and vehicles to create a diversion while the group stole items they required. She crawled through dirt and weeds. Her body smelled but there was no stream to wash properly.

One evening they ran across a small vineyard. Picking a grape, she spit the thing out. The wine didn't taste good either. The men were getting drunk. She was a woman, after all, and the men kept looking at her like she was a siren out for an evening stroll. The woman went towards the bathroom and escaped into the fresh air outside. She hurried around the corner and down the street. A rain barrel was empty, and she climbed inside to sleep the night placing the lid partially over the top. In the morning, she walked back into the terrorist camp.

"Where have you been?"

"Chahaya, I have been ill and didn't want to burden you with my sickness and vomit."

The leader sat down and ate the cooked rabbit he caught. She was given none. Food mattered. Her people placed jerky in small canisters and left them on their planned trail for her to find. She wouldn't go to sleep hungry. The terrorist group was headed in the correct direction. Her accomplices dropped rumors with the appropriate people to spread. The terrorists were hunting one of their enemies or, so they thought.

She knew wooden boxes were being planted and hoped they would be completed in time. In the meantime, she blended into the terrorist group's routine. She became one of them. They stopped at a small stream and she refilled her canteen. Quickly, the woman washed herself. The flies wouldn't bother her anymore.

The men were planning a second major hit. This time six men went on the reconnaissance. She saw the sand hills they would need to walk through. Remembering the map her accomplices drew, she skirted the first box. The men made her take the lead. They stayed a way back from her. If there was anything in the sand, she would be the casualty.

She slowed her stride and passed the second box. The woman looked back at the terrorist cell. They were moving slower. Snake woman didn't fear death. The third box was passed. The hill began to slope downward and there was a small hill and dip. Snake woman looked back once more at the doomed terrorists. They were over one hundred yards back. She gave the all clear signal to the terrorists when she saw her other team lying in wait in the sand, hidden from view.

The terrorists began walking quickly toward her. She repeated their names to herself. Two of them were in the lead. The other three men in the rear fanned outward. The last one fell six feet into the box and disappeared. The second man fell in the second box and disappeared. The third man moved forward and looked back. He didn't see his friends and turned around to look for them. The third man fell into his six-foot box and the box blew upward.

The two lead men were running toward her, swearing in their own language, and firing. Another man hung back. She had already taken cover and was circling back to the third man. Her men waited until the two terrorists came closer. They killed the two lead men easily. She only wore one knife. Her group tossed the extra knives towards her. She brought the last man down. The kill took three knives for he was the largest.

Her crew went back and helped their people out of box one and two. The terrorists were gagged and tied up in the hole. She looked inside each box and repeated the same message.

"You die because my daughter was on Flight 1498. Now your life is mine."

She turned to her accomplice.

"Kill them or I will leave them to the ants."

Her people threw grenades into the boxes, and the other terrorist men were gone.

Snake woman didn't dare go back to the terrorist leader. There was no story that he would believe from her. However, she and her accomplices moved off to set the next trap.

𝕏𝕏𝕏𝕏𝕏

"Chahaya, we have not heard from any of our team. We should investigate the area."

"No, it's the woman. We have run into nothing except bad luck since she joined our camp. There is a reason why she has infiltrated us. We must go back to the town to ask questions. The town's people see and hear things. They will know if strangers are around. The woman, if alive, will be with the strangers. Then we will catch her and torture her to her last breath."

His man said, "She will be placed in the nearest refuse dump."

Chahaya first must catch the woman.

"We must find her. I believe she is a professional who has killed my brethren. Someone put her in our camp as a weapon. We will find out who her backers are, and they will pay."

"But our money is running low. The town's people will want money."

"Tell them we will deliver the money later."

"All right."

"Get going. We need to recruit more people. There are only four of us left."

Weeks went by and there were no rumors or citing of strangers in the area. They picked up two

196

more men to join their group. Their plan was to move to the next town some distance away.

Arriving on the outskirts, the men decided to camp for the evening. Only one man was posted as guard. The campfire was extinguished, and darkness surrounded the small terrorist group.

The next morning, the leader was rudely awakened by a kick to the head. His nose started to bleed. He reached for his rifle which was no longer there. The two new men from town were walking away from the camp. They were, obviously, spies. Then, the leader saw the woman.

"What have you done with my men?"

"Perhaps they catapulted to the moon."

The leader was upset by her flippant response.

"The disappearance of your men should be obvious to you."

"Why have you come here? I don't know you, your leader, or your followers."

"Your assumption is partially correct. You don't know my real name. You do know the person in charge. *I am the leader*."

The man reacted with a deep frown.

"Yes, I thought you would be surprised. This little job is a takedown. Perhaps you have heard of Snake woman in these parts. The snake has come to do a dance because of a story from Chahaya. You bragged to some village men about blowing up an Indonesian airliner. I hate people who brag about killing innocent people."

There was a flicker of fear in the terrorist leader's eyes. He knew who Snake woman was.

"Good, I see you have heard of me. Some people call me a legend. Imagine a smart and highly capable woman. Intelligence and cunning come to mind. The Snake woman kills bad guys. Your name has crossed onto the international hit list. You must know which list that I'm talking about. Your own country wants you terminated. They heard of me and welcomed my challenge to find you. They offered their spies to help me. A well-known, high leader of your country found someone to guide me. However, they told me that I was the master. As a master, I have been granted the power to decide your fate. Your country awaits my decision. They know you have been captured. Now, your job is to follow my procedures."

"What procedures?"

Chahaya was angry with her. She was mocking him. He didn't believe the woman obtained any power. She was the outsider in his country. She was the trickster. Before the Snake woman could throw him more digs, he spoke, "Your mouth will get you killed."

"My mouth? Such absolute nonsense. Here we are having an impromptu meeting. I was talking about procedures and you do riddles. Let's forget what procedure or method will be used. I'm standing here liberated while you are the one bound."

The man looked at his thick ropes.

"Back to our original conversation, the followers have joined me, the nay-sayers have joined me, and the people-on-the-fence have joined me."

She motioned to her accomplice to turn on the recording device.

"There is more that I require. I need the name of the company that created the bomb."

He was fuming and remembered her mentioning the airplane. Perhaps he could explain. There was a reason he chose his path. He tried a different tack because she told him about the others.

"Responsibility belongs to them. What do I care about a plane full of tourists? There was an official on board that someone wanted dead. These people paid me green dollars and gave me the device called NR29. They are the criminals. We needed their money to fund our war efforts. The money was tiny in funds that I received. The company benefited, not me."

"I see. It was too difficult for you to kill one small man. A simple bullet on the street would have worked. A mistake, I'm sure, and the tiny funds."

Suddenly, a thought occurred to Chahaya that he might have made a mistake. "What is the American expression? Yes, I believe you call the passengers collateral damage. Those are the hazards. The company wanted me to make a mistake. Don't you see the problem?"

The Snake woman shook her head.

The man stopped. *She mentioned a method that will be used.* He was starting to get nervous.

The man's pathetic explanation left her feeling cold. The company he talked about provided a type of device which contained a sophisticated miniature trigger. Once released, the device would fire a tiny spiral cylinder which instantly flared like a mini-bomb upon impact, killing one person in an airplane seat if positioned correctly. The device was very small and could be hidden in an airplane tray. Everyone in the international police organizations knew the NR29 was difficult and expensive to purchase. She knew Chahaya switched the bomb and sold the NR29 in the underground market. The homemade bomb he made was the key to massive destruction. His bomb ravaged the length of the cabin, bursting the walls of the airplane for twenty feet. There was no ability to recover. Insanity plunged the airplane to the ocean, devastation, and cold death.

Snake woman came closer and looked him in the eyes. This would be the last time she would stare at his face. Seeing his hatred, she matched her hatred against his.

The prisoner was taken aback. His body stiffened, limbs went limp, and sweat drizzled down his crotch. The hairs stood on his body.

Snake woman grimly continued, "I'm familiar with the NR29 and your avarice in selling the singular device. Your homemade bomb killed much more. Your people are dead like the tourists on the airplane. Everyone, but you, have clumsily fallen into hell. Your men were necessary casualties. Their bodies are mere pieces of themselves. Your twisted evil crew are not coming back to save you."

The prisoner jerkily looked away.

"Nothing has been wasted. Where we could, we saved the clothes, boots, weapons, ammunition, and money. Those items were given back to the towns your crew blew. I've also donated food and water for the people's homes that were destroyed. The supplies should arrive today. Consequently, the only thing left to do is clean-up. You are the last one."

"You shouldn't have killed my men. I might forgive you a bad judgment call and show you some mercy."

The prisoner was not understanding the direness of his situation. Snake woman spoke slowly, "Today is Tuesday. I understand the devil runs a mercy club membership drive on Tuesday. Perhaps you might make the meeting."

Chahaya now understood the craziness of the woman's logic system.

"I can drop my mercy message. I will give you the name of the bomb company. There's no need for clean-up. Let's negotiate."

The Snake woman stopped her pacing. She handed the documents to her team. The terrorist read them, filled in the bomb company name, and signed the documents.

"You will let me go."

She looked at the prisoner. Her answer would surprise him.

"No."

"But I have done what you asked," complained the prisoner.

"If you can generate a miracle and bring the airplane back, I will consent to negotiate. Then we can eat cheese pizza together. Cheese pizza was on the menu per the manifest of food supplies. Then there are the packets of parmesan."

"The airplane is gone with the junk food. What's with the parmesan thing? Your request is impossible."

Snake woman didn't speak. She was hearing her daughter's sweet voice. The voice was a child becoming a woman. The last phone message from her daughter was so clear in her mind. Pain crossed her face for a fraction of an instant.

"Now I see your game. You're the evil one and the last foul woman I will trust."

"I appear to have the upper hand on evil today. You switched the bombs. The final bomb explosion was your fault. You could have done things correctly. We reviewed your actions. The others have now all voted."

"I was forced to sell the special device."

"The decision before my court is that you are guilty. Your avarice for more money was a mistake. The airplane disaster could have been avoided. Enjoy your journey through darkness."

The man struggled as he tried to reach the woman. He was hit in the head again by one of her accomplice's rifle.

"Ow, that hurt. You can't kill me. I did nothing wrong." The man's belligerence wouldn't help him. The countries who supported him withdrew their funds. The man was alone in his deceit and madness.

Snake woman nodded. Her accomplice hit the prisoner again several more times. She held up her hand. The man's face was bloodier. She felt the blood was fitting for the leader's departing look. She wouldn't call the prisoner by his name anymore.

Snake woman motioned to her accomplice and handed him the vial with gloves. Her man took over. She walked past Chahaya.

"My daughter was aboard the downed Indonesian plane. You caused her and the other's deaths."

"No, no, I didn't mean to do the switch in bombs. I didn't trust the other company. That's why we created our own bomb."

The woman stopped. "Really, I believe you now."

The hired, special-painted helicopter landed. Dust settled over the small group. Her group of men would take care of the killer. She withstood enough of this shitty day. Her business was done.

Snake woman gave the signal.

The recorder was turned off. There was no sound and the night was silent. The mamba snake poison was slow-acting. The poison was one of her earlier experiments. The voice box became an inferno and was the first to go. His mouth would kill him.

She walked toward the helicopter and climbed inside. Closing the door, the engine fired up, blades broke the night air, a soft whirring sound lifted the craft, and the woman flew to freedom.

33   Bomb Scare

HIS SECRETARY BROUGHT the package into Derek's conference room.

"The note says to immediately deliver to Mr. Derek Wright."

Derek glanced at the return address. The address was the warehouse in Paris where Jess was jailed by Snake woman.

Rhonda saw his eyes and she immediately jumped out of her chair sending paperwork flying.

"Clear the building, call the bomb squad. Everybody out *now!*"

His secretary pulled the fire alarm and Rhonda called the bomb squad as they ran out of the building. Firetrucks arrived within five minutes. They were on a practice run a few short blocks away.

Derek talked with the firefighters until the bomb people arrived. The robot went in and opened the package. The robot scanned the object.

"The object looks to be a rubic cube or toy. There is a chip, USB object, or something inside. We don't see any explosives, C4, wires or anything. The toy is metal."

Derek looked at the image on the bomb squad's computer. Rhonda peered over his shoulder.

"This is not your normal paint job on the cube. Usually, they are plastic. Someone has painted an image or design on the metal. The item was probably custom-made. I wonder if I can try to solve the puzzle. I'm good with those toys. I play with them to relax."

"She's right. There are several of the things in her office. I can't ever get them to work correct."

"We can get her into some gear and have one of our men be with her."

"Okay, with you?" asked Derek.

"Yes. Do we have a computer we can plug the computer stick into? We don't want to use ours. There could be a video and a virus on the device."

The bomb captain handed Rhonda a small notebook computer.

"Cheap model we use just for this event."

Rhonda and the bomb expert rode the elevator to the top floor in their gear.

She picked up the toy and played with the turns.

"These gloves are making things move slow."

Derek talked into the headset.

"Going slow is fine with us. We're not going anywhere."

"I got it. There's two opposing black images, an airplane image, and a heart exploding. Oh, wait, the item has come apart in two pieces. The USB stick is inside."

The bomb expert motioned to Rhonda.

"We'll put the device in the computer and leave. The robot can start the computer per my technical expert. We're coming down to watch."

The screen showed a dead man's face. The camera panned down to the note on his body.

Chahaya and his terrorists exist no more. Tell the families. The screen played the video and last conversation from Chahaya. The final screen was the signed confession document.

Rhonda took her helmet gear off. She whispered.

"Mother elephant and her raider pack did a terrorist takedown. She obtained a signed confession and killed their leader with the government's permission. Plus, she found the maker of a sophisticated bomb. How bravely brilliant! This person hits high on my scale of one badass female.

Derek nodded. "Insanely crazy. She fought for her revenge, somehow obtaining victory for her daughter plus the other victims and their families."

The bomb experts shook their heads. Their job got stranger every day. They hoped to not see another cube in the next set of bomb calls. They packed their gear. The fire department gave the all clear.

Derek's team re-entered the building. The police removed all items from the conference room. Derek, Rhonda, and Brandon sat down. Derek's secretary brought them fresh cups of coffee. She placed another folder on Derek's table. He looked at her. The secretary walked away.

"Now what?"

34   Akash Disappearance

THE PAPERWORK WAS sent to Derek's department as a courtesy from Mali. He read the report while Rhonda and Brandon waited. Rhonda excused herself to answer a phone call. It was from Skid.

"I saw the news. Are you safe and all right?"

"Yes, sweetheart, everyone is fine. There was no bomb, just a message."

"Snake woman, again."

"Yes, I will talk to you when I get home. I'm in another meeting right now. Let me get back to work."

"Whew. I was scared there for a moment."

Rhonda wasn't sure she was going to tell Skid about her wearing a bomb suit. Maybe she would in a week or two. She went back to their meeting. Derek laid the folder down and clasped his hands.

"There's been an escape in Mali. Akash has disappeared from his brother's house. Evidently, the brother didn't report Akash's absence. He told the police that he thought they took his brother off to jail."

"Oh, man, there goes a potential witness."

"Do you think she had anything to do with his disappearance?"

"We don't know anything. The scene was odd. The front porch was rebuilt by some contractors and landscape of new flowers happened under the policemen's noses. When the police researched the name of the business from a neighbor who saw two trucks, the company doesn't exist."

"I wonder what was under the porch. My grandmother put stuff in jars and hid them in their garden."

Derek and Rhonda looked at Brandon.

"Seriously, she did. However, she left us notes all over the house as to the location."

"I think we might have missed Akash as a criminal. What if he stole some gold?"

"That is too many crazy possibilities in one day," mentioned Derek.

"Getting on another subject, your secretary asked me if you read the psychologist's report. Frankly, I forgot all about the report. The report came in months ago."

"Sorry, Rhonda, the report has been on my desk. I took the folder home. I did this to stop my secretary from bugging me. It's in my office desk in a box."

"We'd like to read the report," said Brandon.

"We should all have a look at the piece. I've read the first page. The psychologist placed the Snake woman's strengths in a grid. The order seemed off to me. That's why I put the report down. She also drew some lines and arrows which made no sense to me. The lines looked familiar. I've been running the image through my mind."

"The image of the words or the lines."

"Brandon, it's a little bit of both. Yesterday, the lines hit me. I remember Shannen's island. There were lines on one of her buildings. The lines are almost a hashtag. The same hashtag is on Matin Domingo's ring."

"The psychologist saw pictures of the ring. She probably thought the marks mattered."

"I know, Rhonda. Anyway, we might want to read the report. I'll have Jess look at the report with me this evening. We'll scan the document to both of you."

"Okay, I'm going home to a worried husband."

"Yes, I'll call Jess. She's heard the commotion by now."

The three players left the building. Derek stopped at the florist to get his wife some flowers. The candy store was next door. He bought her turtle chocolates with pecans and caramel. This was a *just-cause present*. He liked to bring her something on occasion. She enjoyed the treats and special attention. Derek started whistling an opera tune. He had already left the office scene and his investigation work at the office.

He would remember the next day to send the pdf document to Rhonda and Brandon. He wouldn't look at the document for another two weeks. Derek felt there still was nothing there.

In two weeks, Rhonda would talk with Jess to get her perspective. Jess would search and read the document. Her keen eye would pick up a possibility. The arrows showed the movement. Page four revealed the beginning connection between Snake woman and

Matin. The knowledge was something they were looking for.

35 Connection to Matin

DEREK READ THE psychologist report cover to cover. He didn't see anything new. Jess brought him a glass of wine and cheese ball tray. He was glad his wife was wearing the pretty nightgowns again. After the fire, she wore the thick fuzzy robes and slippers because she was cold. Her body temperature had gotten back to normal. He very much liked her this way.

He approached and pulled her into his arms.

"No, not yet. We need to talk first."

Jess tapped the folder.

"You are as determined as my secretary. I've read the thing. We know Snake woman, Margaret, or whatever her name, met and knew Matin Domingo."

"Yes, but there was an attachment. Matin leased Shannen Island before her dummy corporation owned it. What if he gifted the island to her? The island would hold special significance. It would be a hard place to leave permanently."

"I see your point. We can research your idea."

"The ring is important for the hashtag. Look at the psychologist's drawing. You mistakenly believe there is an order or sequence to her weaknesses. She showed them as strengths. There is a change to the order once her daughter is born. The daughter is everything."

"So, murder takes a backseat."

"That's correct. Listen to me roll my idea. The daughter dies, she turns back to murder. Example, kill the terrorist with vengeance. She uses her money to buy mercenaries to help her. Next, she escapes to an island. Which island does she escape to?"

Derek shook his head.

"Your idea is impossible."

"The impossible becomes reality."

"You think she has come full circle and is currently living on Shannen's Island."

"Derek, my idea is worth a look-see trip. You could move Jim's fishing boat there. Maybe ask Simms to join you or the other police officer. You could spy on the island before contacting the police."

"Harry Jenkins from Virginia might be interested in our fishing expedition. Thanks, Jess, I'll give him a call tomorrow. Then I'll run things by Jim."

Jess hugged her smart husband. Derek didn't miss a beat. He was glad they were alone.

"Do we have any oysters in the house?"

"No, but there's a very expensive bottle of champagne in our mini frig."

"Do I have to release you to get the bottle?"

"Yes, but I promise I'll be here when you come back."

Derek touched her hair. Jess was looking at him the way she always did. Her eyes were a beautiful gray like her diamond necklace. He kissed her sweetly and released her temporarily.

Pouring the bubbly liquid into tall crystal glasses, Derek toasted.

"To my dream girl. It was a beautiful day when we ran into each other."

"Yes. My toast is to my knight, my cowboy, and my dreamer boy. And to *cross paths*."

Derek took their glasses and put them on the small table. He twirled her around a few times and bent her over backwards. He slowly brought her up in one more embrace. He hoped her temperature would rise and the nightgown would no longer be a required piece of clothing.

36   Shannen's Circle

THE FOUR MEN were on Jim's fifty-foot boat in the Caribbean. Binoculars were used to see the inhabitants on Shannen's Island. Derek and Harry were down below as the boat trolled past the main house. The two men stayed out of sight for fear the Snake woman would recognize them from Virginia.

The woman in the house was, indeed, looking at the boat with her telescope. She called to her man.

"Akash, the boat in the water. This is the second day in a row the boat has driven by the house. We know the good fishing is on the other side of the island.

"They may not be from around this territory."

"I'm sure you are correct. Strangers mean trouble. Now is the time for us to change living arrangements as agreed."

"I will follow the terms to the letter."

"Thank you, Akash. Please leave me. I have some important calls to make. The catamaran will be arriving early tomorrow morning."

Meanwhile, Jim talked with Derek. The other men were listening on the boat.

"I think we should notify the police and exit the location."

"Jim, we haven't seen anyone other than a gardener on the grounds. We can't see into the house at all. They have special glass installed."

Simms put his two cents in, "I'm all for staying a little longer. The fish fry we had last night was the best I've ever eaten. I didn't know there was a mini barbeque grill for a boat. What a perfectly neat idea! Jim kept that item hidden from me on our last fishing trip."

Jim said, "Well, we were docked in the harbor, and there was no need to cook when a good restaurant was within thirty feet of the boat dock."

Harry rolled his eyes. The voyage had been a fun time getting to know Derek's eccentric friends. He also enjoyed the fish barbeque. There was no leafy green salad anywhere on the boat or protein fruit shakes. Harry didn't take a shower in the morning which for him was unusual. He was enjoying vacation with the boys. His beard was rough and scratchy. He'd sent his wife a text message that they were *roughing it*.

Derek was used to Jim and Simms way of thinking. He was thinking the same thing. Nothing was breaking here at Shannen's Island. He enjoyed himself also, but it was time to leave. They didn't have any reason to storm the island. The men would have one more day of fishing and go home. He sent a note to Jess.

XXXXXX

The next day the men on Jim's fishing boat noticed a flotilla of catamarans approaching the island. Jim lowered his binoculars.

"There looks to be some sort of race happening today. I see a main boat with flags and a sign. They appear to be headed our way."

Derek looked through the binoculars. The timing was not good. He just sent his request to his territorial control people for the coast guard and police assistance. He wanted to hang around when they knocked on the house door.

"This certainly is a strange coincidence. There wasn't anything in the local paper or news. This must be a private organization or club. Can we get them to respond to our radio?"

Harry tried contacting the lead boat.

"They aren't responding. The lead boat has probably turned off their communication device due to the race. We'll have to wait."

"I don't like to wait and am getting an edgy feeling."

Derek looked at Jim. Jim, too, was nervous. Picking up the binoculars, Derek turned towards the house. He saw a spark and a shot crossed their bow.

"Geez, the house is firing at us. Get down below. We are too close. Jim, duck down, and turn the boat away. *Do it now*."

Jim slunk down and peered over the bow as he shoved the controls forward. The boat rose out of the water with two engines at full throttle. It seemed like they were airborne before the boat jolted them to a slower speed when the craft hit the water. The arc driven by Jim moved them away from the island at the boat's top speed. The men held on counting minutes.

Bullets were landing off the stern of the boat until they were out of distance. Jim kept the boat at top speed until Derek gave him further orders.

Derek watched the island.

"We're on the wrong side. Go around to the south where the flotilla is. That's where they will escape."

Jim happily turned the boat. Simms and Harry put bullets in their long scope guns and came to the top of the boat with Derek and Jim. They found metal coolers below and used them as shields. The excitement of chase was happening. None of the men were afraid. They were after criminals.

They saw a catamaran leave Shannen Island in the distance. Harry and Simms pointed at the same time. Their boat was too far away. They saw the catamaran mingle with the other boats. Derek knew something big was happening.

"She's trying to escape amidst the throng of catamarans. Crap, she's staged the flotilla race. I bet she paid for the event and for them to stall for her as cover."

Simms looked at Jim. They were dealing with a planner. Both nodded. The suspect, of course, was a woman. Tricky and fast were in their minds. Harry saw the two men exchange looks.

"There, I see the catamaran. The boat appears to be dead in the water. The sail is down."

Harry looked at Derek.

"I think we need to proceed carefully and keep our distance."

The flotilla of catamarans moved away.

Harry took the lead. "Jim, get closer to the stalled boat."

The one large catamaran was drifting in the water and appeared empty.

Derek received a call from the coast guard. They were twenty minutes out. Derek wanted to board the catamaran. His senses told him to wait.

A lone gun man appeared and took five shots at Jim's boat. Their engine died.

Jim ran to the front of the boat, unlatched, and threw out the anchor. More bullets hit the boat cabin as Jim raced for cover. The anchor dragged in the sand and finally stilled in the ocean.

The gunfire stopped. The men in Jim's boat waited. Stillness was the only option for them. Jim brought out the spear gun and diving gear.

"Do we use this, or do we wait?"

Derek stepped forward.

"I can't ask you to put on diving gear and do this. It was never part of our plan. Besides, there's only three sets of gear and I don't know who knows how to dive other than Jim and me. One of us needs to stay on board."

Both Simms and Harry rose their hands. They knew how to dive. Derek shook his head.

Jim stepped forward.

"Derek, you need to stay and guard my boat. The coast guard will be looking for you personally. You're the man with the answers. We're just your sidekicks. We'll use the high tech underwater cameras and take pictures to send to your computer."

"Are you men all right with the dive and search? If so, maintain high vigilance. We don't know what is out there. But you mustn't disturb the evidence."

Harry stepped forward.

"We're wasting time. I'll take the lead on the search of the catamaran. We'll be fine. We can't lose any more time."

Derek understood. Time was of the essence. No one wanted Snake woman to escape again. Their dingy was lowered into the water. The men jumped inside and started the engine. Jim handed Derek the flare gun.

"Shoot and ask questions later."

Derek opened the side hold and handed Jim the extra shark repellent.

"You do the same."

37   Stranded Catamaran

THE THREE DIVERS approached the catamaran. Two entered the water to look for any explosives underneath. Everything looked normal. Jim went to the front of the boat and dropped the anchor. He looked where the dingy should be on a catamaran. He saw strange metal grooves on the deck under the dingy area's lift. He didn't know what to make of the rails.

The two underwater divers surfaced and climbed back into the dingy. They were going to step onto the catamaran when Jim held up his hand.

Harry said, "Bomb?"

"No, worse. I heard a growl. Let me slide the door a little to the catamaran."

As soon as Jim had a five-inch opening, the dog's nose and large mouth showed. The dog started barking and scratching on the door. Jim jumped into the dingy and the men hightailed it back to Jim's fishing boat. The dog squeezed out the door. Seeing the men in the dingy, the dog jumped into the water and came after them. The men made it aboard when the dog crawled into the dingy.

"Let the rope out. We don't want the dog jumping into our boat."

Harry extended the line.

"Whew, that was close."

Derek contacted the coast guard to notify animal control. The men knew there would be more delay boarding the catamaran. The dog continued barking. Jim went down to the galley and threw two hot dogs into the dingy. The dog wolfed down the bait and sat still.

Jim said, "Now the dog is friendly."

The coast guard arrived, and the coast guard men aboard started laughing. The scene was an unusual one. The dog commandeered the only escape vehicle on Jim's boat. They pulled up beside the stranded craft and rafted together. The men awaited with Derek and the coast guard for the dog rescue boat.

They saw the police boat go around the island to search the house. Derek had been to this place once before and knew there would be nothing.

Derek and Harry went with the coast guard to the catamaran. The two men left on Jim's boat unzipped their wet suits and put their gear away.

Derek saw the device that Jim told him about.

"Will you look at this device on the top here. I'll be darned. The catamaran has some type of watercraft aboard. The grooves look right for a scuba craft to slide so the lift doesn't do all the work. The craft must have been in the water in the center of the catamaran. The sides are built so we couldn't see anything."

The captain of the coast guard looked in the distance. They pulled up the radar screens and didn't see anything either.

"This has to be incorrect. We should see something moving."

The coast guard boat moved away from the catamaran in a wide arc. There still was nothing.

"It's as if the craft has stopped and is waiting on the bottom."

The Coast Guard and police sent out notice in their territory to find two possible criminals from Shannen's Island.

A tow came to pull Jim's fishing boat back to the harbor. The police turned the lights on the catamaran and set lighted temporary buoys around the boat. It was getting dark, and the tow operator would come back in the morning to retrieve the catamaran. The police would continue their investigation and search for fingerprints while the catamaran was moored in the harbor.

During the night, a group of teenagers cut the anchor chain and sailed the catamaran to their own dock where they proceeded to have a party. By the time the police retrieved the vessel, there were thousands of fingerprints, empty beer bottles, and clothes left on the boat. That didn't count the garbage. The teenagers explained they couldn't see the police markings on the buoys because it was too dark. They thought the boat was free-for-the-taking. They planned on renovating the catamaran at a friend's shop.

Derek and his men were disappointed. The search continued for the scuba craft and owner. Derek, Jim, Simms, and Harry flew back home. They knew someone escaped on the scuba craft.

A craft was found on the beach and a dead body. The body belonged to Akash. He wore a gold snake ring. The police made an incorrect assumption. They were under the assumption the man killed himself when there was no other means of escape. The ring was given to Akash as payment for his services, but not services as a lover. Snake woman found someone else. Derek wondered why Akash didn't make it to land. There was plenty of time for him to escape. The police let Derek have their information. There was no license of any kind on the catamaran nor any owner claiming the vessel.

Failure hit the four men. Somehow the woman escaped. All of them felt her presence. Female clothes, makeup, and expensive cologne were found in the house. There was food in the refrigerator.

"She was here."

Jim acknowledged, "And a little too close for my liking."

Jim called a company to repair the bullet holes, and Derek bought him a new red canvas top. Two of the men enjoyed their experience fishing and made plans to go someplace safe. They chose Gig Harbor, Washington.

Derek acknowledged his wife and the psychologist were correct. What they didn't know was the Snake woman was only on Shannen's Island, wrapping up business. The island reverted to her company when the owners missed their last two payments. The man died leaving his wife strapped to make the required amounts on their private loan. The island would be re-sold, and the money squirreled away in an untraceable, off-shore account.

Snake woman moved on to her new adventure and man. Lachlan would sell his interest in his mine in Mali. He would move to America with his riches intact. No one in Mali would care about his departure. He was interested in many of the real estate options presented. He was previewing the state of Washington as his next residence. Lachlan and his new partner wanted a place and environment that was different. They were looking for a surrogate mother. They both wanted a child.

38   Retirement Planning

DEREK WAS DESPONDENT after the trip to the Caribbean. Jess would need to cheer him up.

She bought him a new helicopter. Jess saw the magazines where he circled the models he liked. She talked with Skid and Rhonda extensively about what technical items should be ordered. Skid had been talking to Derek for weeks regarding the new designs. Feeling pretty sure which vessel, he would select, Jess worked with the manufacturer to get the helicopter delivered while Derek was at work.

He came home and parked his sports car in the garage and came through the pool courtyard into the house. He hadn't looked toward the helicopters. Jess was waiting with a blindfold. She made him put the black cloth on and led him back outside.

Standing near the huge machine, she let him take the mask off.

"Jess, oh my god. The helicopter is perfectly beautiful. How did you know?"

He ran over to the new shiny black and silver body, touching the sides lovingly. He jumped in the cockpit.

"Come on, let's go for a ride."

Jess climbed into the other seat. Derek started the rotors and they lifted into the air. They flew past their warehouses and down the ocean beaches and over their yacht. Their captain and crew waved. They knew about the new helicopter. Jess told them.

Flying back to their home, Derek made a smooth, soft landing. He looked at her and gave her a kiss.

"This means you like your present."

Derek laughed.

"Absolutely. Skid and Rhonda must have helped. I wondered why he was grilling me so much about my idea of a perfect machine."

"Let's go back to the house for lunch. You can read the specifications and manuals later. I have an instructor coming to our greenhouse. He's going to show me how to take care of the orchids."

They ate their homemade chicken pot pie with flaky top crust and pea salad. Derek poured them a glass of peach water. He dropped a mint leaf in each glass. Jess grew herbs in her kitchen.

"Let's talk a little bit about the future. I've been thinking about retiring from our investigative services company. I've been talking to people who may potentially want to take over the business."

Jess raised her eyebrows. They talked briefly when she had been injured by smoke inhalation from the fire in Paris. She knew that incident scared her husband more than he wanted to admit. She also worried about their ability to stay out of harm's way which was tightened by the war with Snake woman. Derek didn't want to call his chase a war, but Jess knew differently.

"Rhonda, Tami, and Tiare approached me the other day. They talked to me about the price and how the exchange could be completed with our lawyers.

You must keep this quiet. The women have not yet run any of this interchange through their husbands. Tiare was the one not quite sure of Mic's reaction."

"I think that the three women would be wonderful as a team. Their skills are exceptional and would make a perfect fit. You could always remain in the game as a consultant."

"I was thinking exactly those ideas."

Derek refilled Jess's glass.

"There also is good news about War Julio Samba and his wife, Janet."

"What news? She usually talks to me and I haven't heard anything."

"War Julio has bought a warehouse in Los Angeles harbor. He is expanding his fish business. With the expanded delivery point for his fish and his ability to add fish from the Northwest into his restaurant customer list, he feels more money will flow into his coffers. Plus, Janet wants to be closer to you girls. She misses the female companionship. They will still keep their holdings in Rio and Curacao."

"That is so wonderful news. I know Ara likes Janet. They talk on the phone all the time about kids and being a mom. I can hardly wait. Where are they going to live?"

"They are looking at some land Jack and Ara have which is close to their animal sanctuary where Felidae is buried. I would like to offer our yacht to them while they are here. It should be about three months."

"Excellent ideas. I'm okay with relinquishing our yacht for the three months. The area where they want to build is close to everyone. I'm pleased by all the news. The crony world keeps expanding and the desire to catch the con artist will continue."

"Yes, I knew you are still interested in catching the bad guys. I just want you to be careful if the women proceed. You will need to let them handle things."

"I will."

Derek raised his eyebrows.

Jess picked the lemon out of her glass and sucked on it.

Derek sighed. Jess could be difficult. He leaned over and kissed her lemony mouth. He would have to take her just as she was.

"I'm checking out my new toy. Thank you again."

Derek left Jess with her thoughts. She wasn't thinking about orchids. She was thinking about Mic. Mic would be a good asset. His race car driving skills would be a plus.

"How do we bring Mic into the women's plans?"

The doorbell rang. Her instructor arrived. Jess would have to readdress some ideas later. She let a group of Asian ladies in her home. They brought her a new plant. It was a white phalaenopsis orchid with pink spots. Jess would get to learn all the names of the plants. She was ready to learn.

39   Prison Visit

THE FLIGHT FROM Los Angeles to Phoenix was short. Rhonda drove from the airport to the prison ground and buildings off the I17.

She awaited the prisoner who was in the infirmary. The guard allowed her through several gates and told her she would have ten to twelve minutes with David Remy.

The prisoner was awake and sitting in his bed. The tubes and noises made Rhonda a little squeamish. The man looked pale.

"I'm Rhonda Peters from Los Angeles. They told me it would be all right to ask you some questions regarding your past."

She was told the prisoner was on new medication to control his catatonic episodes. Rhonda pulled out the police photographic drawing of Snake woman.

"Do you know this person? We were told you could possibly be related. She ended up in an orphanage in England. There were stamps on her suitcase, either Jamaica or Bermuda. Her blouse showed the name, Margaret."

The prisoner moved to reach his water. Rhonda helped him.

"Is she alive?"

"Yes, we believe she is very much alive."

The prisoner's eyes watered.

"A strange woman came to see me. I didn't like her. She told me her name was Theresa Tracker and she knew my cousin. We didn't have any cousins, so I didn't talk to her. The strange woman went away. You are the only other person to visit me other than Ms. Quinn."

Rhonda knew about the woman the police called Tracker. This piece of news made her wonder why the woman appeared at the prison.

"Let's get back to the woman in my photograph. We are trying to find out her name and background."

"She was my half-sister. We stole our clothes. We stole lots of items to survive. She could steal better than me. Her knowledge of machines was excellent. She hot-wired the first car we stole. We were a team. I lost her when we were in England and couldn't find her again. I believe she ran into some men who were in the neighborhood we were in. I tried to find her, gave up, and came to America. She was very *resilient*. I knew she would adapt. The street people and savages never scared her. Nothing scared her after she spent time in the closet. Then I got into some bad people and my life went south from there."

"Your file shows your father as Jackson Remy. He was a special ops person and moved to Oregon where he was a leader of a gang. They were into anti-American values. I'm surprised you came back to the states. Did you and your half-sister live here?"

"I liked America until I got caught. I wasn't like my father and his politics. We did initially live in

Oregon, except my father broke away from the group. She probably was too little to remember the beach in Oregon. We used to try to skip stones in the ocean near Cannon Beach. I don't know why my father left the area. His decision changed everything for us. We traveled to Jamaica and Bermuda for some time. He was very strict with us. Our education was 24/7. My half-sister and I are very smart. He took advantage of our intelligence which probably was a good thing. Once the hurricane hit, we were on our own. His camp was totally wiped out and he was gone. We survived by climbing trees. Earlier we made a fort out of the palm leaves. She wove them together real tight. She learned from an elderly woman in the village. The branches mostly held and somehow gave us adequate cover. Her skill saved my life. We hopped a freighter and made our way to London. London was another bad decision which I regret."

The man started coughing and the nurse came in. She motioned five minutes left.

"Your half-sister, what was her mother's name and her name? It's important. We need to locate her."

The prisoner frowned. Perhaps he told too much information. He knew his sickness was close, and there wasn't much time left. He was glad someone was looking for his half-sister, yet he worried. The police used information. Would his sister want him to divulge any more? He didn't know if this woman wanted to hurt her. The Tracker person most certainly did.

Rhonda immediately saw a change in the man and watched as he started to vacillate about their interview. She saw him shut down.

"Please."

The man stirred.

"The police have the list of names from the *Comet* organization in Oregon. My mother and her mother's names are there."

The guard came into the room. It was time for Rhonda to leave. The prisoner, David Remy, was asleep from the morphine. She had no choice but to end their interview. She hoped the list of names from Oregon would be helpful. The prisoner was helpful. He gave Rhonda valuable data.

"Thank you, Rosemary Quinn, for the hints pointing us in this man's direction."

Rhonda flew back to LA. The Oregon police didn't have any list of the women in the camp because there were no arrest records for them. Rhonda asked if she could see any files or data the police captured from a raid. The raid was a month after Jackson Remy's departure. The files were worth exploring.

In Oregon, Rhonda sat in the special room for reading case files. There was no information about the women in the camp. She was disappointed. Rhonda checked through the recorder of record's office and there didn't appear to be any birth certificate for a female child by Jackson Remy. The reason might have been an easy one. The mother of Snake woman didn't record the father on the birth certificate. There also was a mid-wife who lived in the camp to deliver any babies. Therefore, there would be no hospital records.

She went out to the now defunct camp. Walking the grounds, she saw massive and extensive military-style training grounds. The work-out each day to drill through the exercise course must have developed muscles. There was a school room for the children which looked directly onto the course. The children saw the training of their peers every day. The place creeped Rhonda out. At the end of the course was a small billboard sign. Evidently, paper pictures were placed upon the board. There were odd hashtag marks on top of the board.

Rhonda knew the hashtags represented winners.

"The ring, Matin Domingo's ring. She included the hashtags because he was a winner. He was her winner. I think that I get that concept. He was the first thing good in her life. The only thing was that she found out later. Matin was a smuggler. He was in to evil. Not a good thing at all. She left him."

Rhonda felt she was almost touching something. She saw the suspect as a young child. Her life was miserable. The way the young child grew up was horrible. Something resonated from Rosemary Quinn, the psychologist.

Snake woman creates barriers. She only allows you to see what she wants. She controls everything.

The back of the sign went unnoticed. Had Rhonda looked, there was a child's carving of a single word. The word was almost invisible now because the child's tool wasn't very sharp. The word meant everything. It said, *lucky*.

Rhonda was clueless. She was at a loss. The police were chasing an illusion. They were chasing a ghost. There was nothing further in Oregon. She was at another dead end in finding Snake woman's real name or her mother's name. With the real name, the police could possibly find someone who knew the woman and catch her.

Rhonda called the prison to arrange another meeting with David. She needed more information to solve the puzzle. The prison informed Rhonda that he passed away.

"Another bust and dead end."

40   Gig Harbor

JIM MICHAELS AND Simms were on the rental fishing boat. They were at a rental house and the boat was moored off the dock. The two men decided they would check out as many harbors, inlets, bays, etc. for the rest of their lives. Fishing was important. It wasn't the protein so much as the thrill of the game. They were both retired from the police life. Jim only did occasional work for Derek. There was a younger person, Brandon, that took over Jim's duties.

There was a party across the harbor. The noise level was getting a little higher. Jim worried the noise would scare the fish off.

Jim went back to the house to get more beer and make some ham salad sandwiches. Stuffing everything in a plastic carry bag, Jim stepped onto the dock.

Simms was staring across the water at the party.

"Let's take a break until the party noise diminishes."

Jim deposited the plastic bag on the swing table, went to his rod, and reeled in the line. Simms did the same. Jim opened the bag and passed out their lunch. The chips were passed to Simms.

"What? No dip?"

Jim made a move to get up.

"It's all right. I can live without the dip."

"Are you sure? The plastic label showed guacamole, extra hot."

"Go, go get the guac and mustard."

Jim stepped off the boat and went to the kitchen. Grabbing the dip, jar of bread and butter pickles, and squeeze bottle of mustard, he stopped.

There was a woman across the way that looked familiar. Jim kept staring and the woman turned.

Jim said to himself. "Oh, man, it's her."

He slowly moved toward the rental boat. Jim handed the dip to Simms's awaiting hand and he put the jar down. The squeeze bottle was tossed to Simms. Jim sat and picked up his beer. He looked at anything other than the woman across the way. Simms kept scooping out a large portion of the green goo onto his paper plate. Next, he squeezed yellow mustard on the ham sandwich. Nothing came out. Simms unscrewed the cap. His friend forgot to take the white seal off. He resealed the cap and a thick layer of mustard came out.

Simms noticed Jim was quieter than normal. Usually, Jim complained about the amount of mustard he used. There was no agitated comment. He looked at Jim slowly eating the sandwich. Jim usually wolfed down food.

"Nice day, don't you think?

There was no response from Jim. He tried again.

"Hickory, dickory, dock is my favorite rhyme. It's this dock that made me think of silliness. I don't usually do music when I'm fishing. The fish don't like drums. Now, me, drums work fine."

Simms took the can of beer, tapping the Formica, and singing the silly song. He picked up a large bobber.

Jim hadn't heard him. Simms glanced across the harbor at the party group. He didn't see anyone there that he knew. Simms opened the pickle jar and put ten on his plate. He threw the bobber at Jim. Jim fumbled, but caught the red and white plastic object.

"Would you like some pickles, Jim?"

"What, oh, yeah, give me some pickles."

Simms was glad his friend was back. He hoped the man wasn't getting some old person's disease.

"Where did you go just now?"

Jim sighed.

"I was making an important decision."

"Do you want to talk about it? Perhaps I can help, my friend." Simms touched Jim's hand.

Jim started talking.

"I have friends who are in the police business. One of them recently got hurt and the other one sometime before that. There's this bad person they keep chasing. I think I've seen something."

"The something is the bad person, and you saw her across the way? Is it the Norway Pine?

"You're very perceptive."

"This means that I should keep talking and not look at people at the party. Our friends are Jess and Derek."

"Correct on every scale. The bad person always has an exit plan."

"I remember her powerful telescope, not to mention the flotilla of catamarans. Then there's the bullet holes in your boat."

"Yeah, you're catching onto my story and dilemma."

"You believe she is still watching us and recognized who we are? We're in danger. I've read her list of possible crimes. Real scary broad."

"Yes, to all questions. My hat and your mustache haven't changed since the last time she saw us. It's probably my shiny lure that caught her attention. Plus, there's our association to Derek and the other cop onboard."

Simms looked at Jim's hat.

"No doubt about it."

Simms picked up his sunglasses to stop the glare from the lures and water. Simms wished he could rewind this morning back to the start. Everything in his world had been peaceful. They were in a sweet cove listening to the birds and saw an occasional fish jump. Then the party started and destroyed the quiet. Next, the woman appeared. Women criminals were the worst. Their unpredictable nature meant difficult. Simms didn't want to do difficult today. Obviously, neither did Jim. However, he was a retired cop and so was his friend. He finished his beer and crushed the can.

"How fast do you think we could get this rental tub started?"

"Not fast enough," said Jim.

"There's our guns."

"Still, not fast enough."

Simms had to ask, "What if this time she doesn't have a plan?

"This woman is the ultimate Queen of plans. Piss poor is not in her vocabulary. She wrote the manual on escape. Resilient as all hell fits. Dean Crain wouldn't take the bet. He always knew when the odds were stacked against him. He was the King of poker."

Simms rubbed his mustache. He knew Dean Crain. Simms saw him one time in Las Vegas on the casino floor.

"Did I tell you about my first meeting with Dean? If not, here goes the story. Dean saw a dealer he knew in Vegas who spun the roulette wheel at the club. Now I don't play the wheel because of the green zero and double zero. Those two buckets make me lose, but then maybe I'm playing the wrong game. Anyway, on a lark, he places his bet. The dealer throws the wheel. Dean won and walked away. At the bar, I introduced myself, and he remembered me from the Napa case. That's when he let me in on his secret. This dealer spins the wheel with the same force every time. Dean knew the odds of the numbers the balls always landed with the dealer. He always bet. The house moved the dealer around, believing the wheels were the problem. The dealer and his skill broke the house."

Jim looked pensive and spoke. "There was this song about holding or folding. Dean knew when to fold. We should fold. There's always another card game."

He agreed with Jim that any movement was too risky. Besides the rental on the boat didn't include bullet holes. Plus, there were the pedestrians at the party. The hazards were too great.

Jim finished his beer and handed the can to Simms who crushed it. Simms tossed both cans down the opening into the boat galley. The other beer cans were on the floor. They bought a green grass rug at the bait store. The rug kept the cans stationary, so they didn't make noise when the boat rolled around. The best part was their ability to hose the fake grass rug down.

The men also drank too much beer yesterday. Their aim might be off. Earlier, they placed their guns in holsters on the bench table down below. The loaded bullet clips were next to the guns. The men were always prepared for a little trouble while fishing. Sometimes boaters came a little too close. Usually, it was the bad dudes with extra testosterone in a fast speed boat. Jim and Simms didn't take kindly to speeders rocking their turf. Their rifles with scopes were in the trunk of the car. It was too late to get those weapons.

There was no more response from Jim.

"Yes, sir, I think we ought to stay and fish some more. I forgot to tell you that I entered us in the fishing contest when I bought the dried squid bait. The squid was expensive. I do believe we could give the fishermen in these parts a run for their money now we have obtained the special bait. The reason it's so special is a question you should ask."

The mention of the contest made Jim relax. It was a good distraction technique for his frayed nerves.

"What's so special about this squid and you bought some fresh shrimp?"

"The bait is taken directly out of this harbor. Some guy grows the stuff on a fish farm."

"The squid?"

"No, no. The water here is fresher. I'm talking about the shrimp. Occasionally, the fish farm people toss the half-dead shrimp overboard. They're not supposed to do that. They are lazy and figure, what the heck? Dead or almost dead works for them. Fish will eat the pieces of shrimp and save the environment. So, you see, the fish in this water are familiar with the tasty morsel. Then we get to the dried squid."

Jim grinned. Simms was full of riddles. The word dead or almost dead was close to their situation.

"Again, why did we buy squid?"

"To put inside the shrimp. The taste is a double wham of delight."

"Delightful," said Jim while scratching his head and tilting his hat. His sunglasses were back at the house. Jim would have to wait to get them.

Only Simms could ratchet-jaw with the locals and get a story out of the deal.

Both men got their lines and gigs ready. They tossed out the lines in the same spot they were previously. The men sat down. They made a pact to not disclose the location to the Wrights just yet.

Suddenly, a large fish yanked Jim's line and the men were busy with net trying to pull the fighter fish onto the boat. They were excitedly hollering at each other and telling the other person what to do next. The Snake woman was forgotten. She wasn't their prize today.

The woman across the way moved from the huge Norfolk pine. The potted plant screened her image. The image was there and not there. Her dress blended with the branches. Today, she was brave and wore a snake skin fabric. The party was an invite from a guest at their hotel. On a whim, she decided to attend. Closely monitoring the two fishermen's activity, her suspicious mind relaxed a fraction. The men hadn't recognized her. She watched them struggle with the huge fish.

"Two strange blokes, indeed."

Her man came alongside and looked across at the fishermen. He was there to drive her back to the hotel. He was ready to leave because the car was waiting in a loading zone. They walked together, exiting the party. She drove him back to Seattle for his flight. They made plans to meet in the future. Her plans were to buy a home around these islands.

Seeing the two fishermen changed her plan. She would look for a different location. Her friend would be agreeable. They would find escape in a beachfront property. Sand and water were her favorite place to reside. Walking on the beach brought her happy memories. She had taken her daughter on vacations there. Memories were pushed to the back. Her old way of life was already forgotten. She would leave the old fishermen alone.

41   Tami and Jess

THEIR NEW BUTLER let Tami Cortez into the Wright's living room. Jess entered the room and hugged Tami.

"Who is the doorbell guy?"

Jess waved her hands.

"It's Derek. He bought me a three-month package to try out a butler. This house is so big. I sometimes don't hear the door or the guard gate call. I put my new earphones on and listen to music. Therefore, people are kept standing outside here or at the gate."

"By the way, I do love your new digs. I am here to ask a favor. It's Tiare. She wants to join us with our new business venture. Mic has put up a massive roadblock or something equivalent to a stockade to keep her away from the clutches of Snake woman."

"So, he's worried about the woman crashing down their perfectly fine life."

"Yes. He knows Tiare is unhappy working for the police. She is bored and wants more challenges. Mic wants her to stay where she is."

"Oh, dear. That could lead to trouble for them. Tiare is pretty and a redhead. Her temper is headstrong at times and, I might add, determined. We know who she is inside and out. Has she talked with Derek about this issue?"

"I'm worried about them as a couple, too. No, Tiare didn't want to bother either of you. I have no qualms asking for your help. I figured that between the two of you, the better negotiating skills with a man resided with my dear friend, Jess. I think it's because we females have a connection. I love Derek, but he doesn't always know us."

"Thanks. Tami, you have a very keen sense of direction in finding female support. Yes, Derek, would help you. However, I have insights and connections he does not have. You were correct in approaching me. Besides, Derek is wrapped up with the business portion. How do you propose I get Mic alone without Tiare around?"

"I was thinking that you could deliver a new orchid from your greenhouse tomorrow. I know Tiare is working and Mic will be tinkering with his new race car at home."

"Let me have some time to decide my plan of attack and get the bouquet ready."

"Color me gone. I'll let myself out."

Jess went to her den to think. She remembered Dean's arguments to her when Derek wasn't cooperating. She wondered if any of them would work.

The next day, she walked into Mic's five car garage. He was fooling around with the car engine. He saw her and wiped his hands on a clean rag.

"Jess, what a pleasant surprise. I see your magic fingers have grown an orchid. My wife likes these but kills them fast."

"Don't worry, I put a small feeder tube inside, and the container lights up when it gets too dry."

"Now, a lighted pot is cool."

Jess decided to be honest in her approach.

"I wanted to talk to you about Tiare while you and I were alone. It's work related."

Mic shook his head.

"There's no room in changing my mind."

"Perhaps you can listen to a wiser woman who knows Tiare longer than you."

Mic knew he was in trouble. The word wiser rankled. Tiare used the same word on him.

"Let's go to the patio where it's more comfortable. I'll get us some water."

Mic and Jess sat down. "Okay, shoot."

"I have an idea that you have run into problems with Tiare's decision to become a police woman. She was not the type of woman that you usually choose for a date or would marry. However, her strong opinion and skills were what drew you both together."

Mic knew his love for Tiare was much more. "You are correct. She does crazy stuff like climbing hotel walls with a rope to get into the place."

"And you do crazy things like race car driving on roads in Florida with boars and alligators."

Jess saw Mic's expression of disbelief.

"I have my sources at the track. They love to tell stories."

"You mean the announcers?"

"No, but obviously a competitor."

Mic knew the competitor was Dan. He groaned.

"Tiare and I are the same personality type. That is what you are trying to explain to me. Okay, I get it. What do you propose we do about a huge knot of contention between us? I'm exhausted and going in circles. I see her unhappiness. She comes late to bed. I can't take the stress."

Jess was glad Mic asked for her help. It was a step forward.

"Why not come to a temporary solution?"

Jess almost said the word, truce. Truce was something she wanted the two people to work on together.

Mic began to look worried.

"Let her take a leave of absence from her job, probably six months. Next, allow her to join the team of investigative personnel with Tami, Rhonda, and Brandon for the six-month period. Let her see if this is what she really wants in her career. It would give both of you time. We could make a secret stipulation in the verbal part of the contract that Tiare is not available to work on any case connected to Snake woman."

"Now your idea is pushy, but very shrewd."

Jess wanted to hit Mic over the head. He hadn't even run into her power of push. She had been gentle. Derek would have seen all the signals that Jess sent out when her energy flashed fire and fueled a chase of criminals. He would have told Mic to duck.

Calmly, taking her water bottle, Jess left Mic at the patio table.

Mic was so surprised, he didn't know what to do. He almost called out goodbye and thought better of it.

The game just changed. With Jess on Tiare's side, all the other crony women would follow. Suddenly, Mic found the connection, Jess was the Queen bee of an entire enclave of women. He knew if his wife found out about the lockdown he placed on her career, there would be hell to pay. He thought of Oymyakon, Russia, where the temperatures dropped below minus fifty degrees Fahrenheit. Tiare could go colder than that were his thoughts. Mic would be the odd person standing, the tyrant. The women were the power players.

Everything about Tiare was now clear. She belonged to their sphere of influence. He didn't really know his wife that well. He needed to step aside and let Tiare confront her dream. His support and love were what she wanted. He would try to relinquish control. His marriage wasn't the race. There were two of them steering the race car. At least, there would be the secret pact about Snake woman. He could explain that piece away if his wife caught on. Still, Mic was confused. He would talk with Derek to get reinforcements.

Mic went into the house to take a shower. He waited until his beautiful wife came home. He made her dinner. The dinner was a hot egg sandwich with bacon, tomatoes, and lettuce. Tiare was apprehensive. They put the dishes in the dishwasher together.

Mic took her hand and steered her into their bedroom to talk. He told Tiare the plan they should follow. He didn't tell her the idea was Jess's. She hadn't yet seen the orchid left on the patio table.

"Oh, Mic, I like the idea of six months. I'm ecstatic with delight."

She jumped into his lap and started kissing him. Mic couldn't believe the change in her attitude. He felt he made the right decision. Now there would be peace in his house.

The next morning, Tiare contacted Derek to start her contract paperwork. She gave notice with her police captain.

Tami and Tiare bought a new glass window with Tiare Palla's name in white etched letters. The glass would be installed after the contract was approved.

42   New Name

THE THREE WOMEN were gathered in Derek's office. Brandon was out for the day with the flu. He gave his vote on a new name to Derek.

"Tami, Tiare, and Rhonda. Congratulations on your new contract as private investigators. The last item we must do is the name change on the firm. Then we can order the new badges and alert our security department."

The women excitedly looked at each other. They didn't know they could choose the new name.

"Rhonda has our current files that we are working. She will be the liaison to assign the work and the new leader of your group. If there are any questions, she is the person you need to contact. Brandon will be your second contact. My secretary will provide you with any necessary items. Your furniture and offices are ready."

Derek nodded at Rhonda to take the floor. He would step out for an hour to let them work on the name.

"Well, girls, here we are together at last. It will be my pleasure to work with you. Tami and I have history and have worked with each other in the past. Brandon also is invaluable in this office. Like Derek told us, he can help smooth your way. The police contact information will go through my desk. We give them what we can, but our clients take priority. Enough of my speech. Let's put our heads together."

The girls kept going back and forth of the name. Finally, they gave up and placed Jess on the speaker phone. They didn't know that Jess heard rumors about Brandon moving to New York. He had family there and would be leaving in three months. Derek hadn't told them.

"Hi, Jess, we have several names and are undecided. We thought you could help us with the task at hand."

"I'll try my best. Congratulations, Tiare, it's good to see your new window. The girls sent me a photo via text."

"Thank you Jess for the orchids. I found them the next day."

Tami looked at Rhonda and winked.

"We all like the word, force. We've tried power force investigations, force four investigations, power house investigations, and LA force investigations. None of these seem an exact fit."

Jess said, "How about LA Tri-Force Investigations?"

Tiare looked around the table. Tami and Rhonda knew something she didn't. Tiare thought it was her. She thought she would be out.

Jess saw her confusion on her monitor and wondered if she should disclose information.

Rhonda didn't want Tiare to feel out of the game.

"Brandon may be leaving us."

The look of relief was worth the disclosure. Rhonda was up to handling Derek's disapproval. This wasn't the first time Rhonda moved in her own direction. She believed that was why Derek hired her and Tami. Derek liked women who spoke their mind. He even admitted to being wrong on occasion. Yet, most of the time, Derek made the call and hit the answer to their problem on the nose.

"Girls, what is your vote?"

They shouted the name at once, *LA Tri-Force Investigations.*

Derek stepped back into the room.

"Hi, honey, isn't this a cozy meeting that I missed?"

Jess smiled and talked briefly with Derek. She was going with the twins to visit the tiger cages at the zoo.

The women in the room smiled and the call was over.

"I believe the entire office heard the new name. I'll contact our lawyers. Now, if you don't mind, I'm going to the zoo to surprise my family. I need a break and suggest you do the same. Tomorrow is early enough to begin work."

Derek shook his partners' hands.

Riding in his sports car, he remembered. The zoo concession served hot dogs. He hadn't eaten hot dogs in some time. The cheese and garlic fries sounded good to him. He stepped on the gas.

Jess and his daughters were at the exhibit blowing kisses to the tigers. The brother and sister were separated now into their own areas. Every now and then, the male tiger would call out. The sister cat would reply. Ara and Jack Jones had brought her tiger, Felidae here. The two cats were his offspring.

Derek approached Jess and gave her a hug. His daughters began telling him about their day. Life was very good indeed.

43   Mine Owners

THE WEATHER WAS perfect for golf. Derek walked into Rhonda's office. She looked up and grinned.

"Nice legs."

Derek wore shorts and a golf shirt.

"I could respond in kind, but my wife would frown. The Mali police interviews are finally here on the two mine owners."

"Do you want to read the lengthy report or receive a recap from me?"

"Go ahead, Rhonda."

"There are only the two large mines in the area and many small holes in the ground that the locals dig without a license. The two major players in the gold industry are Bryce Hatcher and Lachlan Thomas. Mr. Hatcher admitted to a longstanding, exclusive affair with Danielle Ashley. There hasn't been any theft recently on his property. When someone steals from him, his company turns the thief over to the authorities. Mr. Hatcher explained to the police his failure at recognizing character flaws about his paramour. Never once did he believe she would smuggle gold out of the country. Anyway, that is what he is professing. He told the police that he bought Danielle many pieces of expensive jewelry and would have given her gold had she asked him."

Derek shook his head.

"The man loves her and is covering for her. Tell me about Lachlan. He sounds Irish which seems like a coincidence."

Mr. Thomas has been out of the country and just returned. This is the reason for the delay in the report. Evidently, he has been trying to sell the mine for over a year."

"Do we know where Lachlan has been?"

"His passport shows Hong Kong and Seattle."

"Another coincidence. Hong Kong is where the daughter was traveling to. And what business would the man have in Seattle?"

Mr. Thomas owns an extravagant condominium in Hong Kong and frequently travels there. The flight to Seattle was to meet the investors who recently purchased the mine. The gold was declining and would require heavier equipment which Mr. Thomas did not want to invest. The security at his complex is tight and there were no recent incidences reported of theft."

"In other words, we are at an impasse."

Rhonda drank her water.

"Not necessarily. The police questioned a hotel in Mali where Mr. Thomas frequented. He reserved the conference room frequently. It was the same conference room that they saw Ms. Ashley enter."

"Ah, a tryst or a business engagement."

"The Mali police believe the two people were having an affair."

"She wasn't exclusive. I wonder what Mr. Hatcher would think of this revelation. I'm sure he would change his mind about the jewelry and gold statement."

"Mr. Thomas was surprised about the gold smuggling."

"I bet he was," said Derek.

Derek looked out the window at the LA traffic.

"Do we have an address for Lachlan?"

"Yes, we have the address on the condominium and a post office box in Mali. He still owns a house there. The house wasn't part of the mine sale that we know. The police were told that Mr. Thomas will be traveling to view his favorite escape destinations next year. The man has worked ten years non-stop and wants some play time. Mr. Hatcher has no plans to leave the area permanently. We might think otherwise about these two men and follow their status later."

Rhonda let Derek mull over her summary.

"There's one more item in the report on Akash's brother. Per the brother, Akash didn't know how to swim or dive. Danielle's company paid for a life insurance policy on Akash. Hence, the brother received fifty-thousand dollars."

"Isn't the amount higher than usual for a company, especially one in Africa."

"The amount appears odd, except the insurance is real and legal. The police have chosen no further action against the two living mine company men or Akash's brother. They've closed the case. Do you want me to keep the file open or closed?"

"Let's mark it *Unresolved File*. Snake woman has disappeared. We can consider the men further when she reappears."

Rhonda stepped out with the file to deliver the item to their secretary.

Derek wondered about the snake ring they found on Akash.

Derek thought to himself, "The ring was part of a smoke and mirrors game. She never parted with the memento until now. The question was why? Rhonda said the ring was a key. Unless there are two rings? This logic makes more sense to me. If so, which of the two men has the second ring? One of the men may be involved. There is no proof. Someday there will be evidence."

He removed himself from Rhonda's office and went to his golf game. Derek was going to *escape*. It was easier this time to walk away.

XXXXXX

Mary Beth, Jim's wife, found a picture of Simms and her husband on a fishing trip. The men entered a fishing contest and won the largest fish of the day. Both men wore new hats that read Gig Harbor. The hats were the prize and a check for one hundred dollars. Mary Beth smiled remembering how happy Jim was when he came home. Flipping the photo over, she was surprised to see the words written in Jim's hand. The words were *Cross Paths, Snake woman*.

She wondered about the words. Jim was in a nursing home following a slight stroke. However, he was on the mend. She expected him home after he recovered. Driving to Rhonda's office, she stopped in the parking lot. Tiare came over to talk with Mary Beth. Mary Beth handed the photo to Tiare to deliver to Rhonda.

Tiare, naturally, opened the envelope and read the words. The words could be the lead they were looking for. She pocketed the photo and went into their building. She wanted to be part of the investigation. The photo was her bargaining chip to persuade Tami and Rhonda to let her into the chase game.

44   Brita Encounter

BRITA WAS TOLD to stay in place until a message came from Ms. Ashley. She would receive a packet of instructions and airline tickets. One of those tickets would be for a visit to her sister. A new set of luggage was delivered to her the other day. The luggage was for her trip. A new passport was tucked inside the small case.

Brita used the last batch of eggs from the refrigerator to make a custard pie. She took the hot pie plate out of the oven and placed the object on the bread board to cool. The pie was for later. She and the chef were having a treat along with slices of fried chicken.

Then she went out to the garden to pick kale, turnips, and a rutabaga for the chicken soup the chef would make. The soup would be frozen until Mr. Hatcher's return. The man loved the crazy stuff and ate the soup for lunch. Brita didn't like the turnips nor the rutabagas.

After digging the vegetables, she went to the small shed to wash them. Throwing the leftover tops into the compost bin, she dug out her phone. The phone was new and sent to her by Ms. Ashley. She kept the phone with her and always put the device on silent. Brita could only use the phone when she was away from the house and there was an emergency. She smelled the vegetables and frowned.

"Turnips were disgusting. Rutabagas were even worse."

They reminded her of pigs. The gas was the problem. After eating the tops of both vegetables, the pig's stink in the air quadrupled from their belly full of gas.

"There's enough gas to light a flame thrower before the shit storm. Nope, there won't be any turnips or rutabagas in my garden in America. We'll have solid white and red potatoes."

She dropped the vegetables on the counter in the kitchen and the chef started peeling them. The doorbell rang, and the woman dried her hands to answer the door.

Two white men stood on the threshold. Brita said, "We don't need any religious pamphlets today."

One of the men turned and she saw the airport limousine.

"Are you lost?"

"No, maam, we wondered if Mr. Hatcher was home. We went to the mine and was told that he might be here."

"The mine people would never send you to his house. They know better."

The two strange men looked at each other. This broad looked stupid.

"We are the Madden brothers and would like to speak to Mr. Hatcher."

"The mine people should have told you he is out of the office."

"They did say he would be gone for five days."

Brita was tired of talking to the men playing a game of riddles. It was her job to turn the tables.

"Madden, is that spelled M. a. d. u. n?"

"No, we are Barry and Gerard M. a. d. d. e. n from America. If you would let Mr. Hatcher know we called, we could meet with him."

"North or South?"

"Pardon me, maam. What do you mean?"

"North or South?"

"Oh, North America."

"That's a huge place," said Brita.

"We're from Miami." Barry handed her his business card.

Brita pocketed the card in her apron without looking at it.

"You wouldn't by any chance know Ms. Ashley or where she has gone on vacation?"

Brita was surprised by their question. There was something fishy about these two men. The stink around them was getting higher.

"I work in the garden, kitchen, and go to the store. I don't see people like Ms. Ashley."

"Maybe you know of one of her acquaintances? We certainly would appreciate the help."

"I work in the garden, kitchen, and go to the store. I don't see people."

The two men looked at each other again. Gerard stepped forward, getting close to Brita's face. He pocketed his hand in his suit. Brita didn't move an inch.

"You must have a name, just one little name will do. Then we can be on our way."

Brita played the game.

"I work in the garden, kitchen, and go . . ."

She stopped talking because Gerard held up his hand.

"We believe you. Just give the card to Mr. Hatcher."

In disgust, the two men walked away and stepped into the airport limo.

Brita was skeptical when she saw Barry get in the driver's seat. She looked at the business card which said lawyer. Two lawyers driving an airport limo in Africa.

"Well, that's a new one."

She wondered. She fingered her lighter. If she threw it towards the vehicle, she knew the obnoxious gas fumes would ignite.

"Bag of gaseous wind are what those two blokes are about. They don't know half the trouble they're in." Brita went into the kitchen. The chef was scurrying around making a list of groceries. He looked wild-eyed and frantic.

"You must go to the store, Brita. The gardener will drive you because your beater car might not make the trip. Anyway, I don't trust the thing and we must be constantly prepared. We need more eggs, frozen strawberries, whipped cream, and bread. Oh, also a roast for tomorrow. Flour, we need more flour for dumplings. Here's the list. Mr. Hatcher will be home shortly. His dentist canceled the appointment. Mr.

Hatcher won't be in a good mood unless he has strawberry shortcake."

Brita hurried to the store with the gardener waiting in the truck. Stepping outside the back of the store, she made her phone call to Ms. Ashley. She told her about the two strange men, their names, address, and phone number, and the fact that Mr. Hatcher was returning earlier than planned.

"Thank you, Brita, for the call. These two men are not our friends. You've assessed the scene correctly. Please destroy their card. I will handle things on my end. There will be a bonus for today. This was an emergency. Now, go about your business."

The caller hung up and Brita did the same. She took her lighter out of the other pocket and lit her cigarette.

"Girl, you know how to wrap your brain around fakes."

She patted herself on the back for doing a good job. Her boss knew and appreciated her intelligence. The air smelled better now. There was no eggshell smell. Brita lit the Miami lawyer's business card with her cigarette and watched the paper disappear.

45   Tami's Case

THE CELL PHONE rang, and Derek grabbed it off the desk. The call was Tami Cortez. She didn't want to bother Derek this soon on her new job, except there was something strange about her case. She exhausted all avenues and wasn't sure which direction to pursue. Tami thought about her friend, Rhonda, but she looked busy working her set of cases.

"Derek, here."

"Hi, do you remember the case assigned to me regarding the woman, Stephanie Crandall?"

"I do, what's up with her case?"

"Well, her husband died, and she asked us to review the police files which I did. Her husband was run off the road by a white van and died from a head wound which they assumed was from the accident. The police never found the van. The man has been dead two years. Mrs. Crandall thought nothing of the head wound until she saw a fight that her son recorded on his computer. The fighter punched the man in the same location of the head as her husband was hit. The wounded fighter went down and died from a severe concussion. She thought perhaps her husband was murdered the same way. When she talked to her son about the fight video, he just shrugged and told her she was being silly."

"I assume you have seen the fight tape and police photos?"

"The blow to the head and wound look similar. There is a high probability the husband was murdered. The ability to convince the police was slim. Then, a new development has occurred. Mrs. Crandall went on vacation, flew to Peru, checked out her rental car, and arrived at the hotel. The Peruvian authorities found the rental car at the hotel and no Mrs. Crandall. She told the desk she was taking a scenic bus ride.

"People disappear all the time in Mexico and South American countries."

"I know, but there's a newer twist. The FBI is at the scene."

"Did you talk with the FBI?"

"I did, and they told me the case is classified."

"The possibility exists for spy espionage with the husband and wife or illegal, heavy-duty dealings."

"Yes, I'm afraid so. Normally, we sit back and let them take over."

"That would be my same conclusion with this case," said Derek.

"Unfortunately, there's a problem. The man's daughter from a previous marriage wants to hire us to find her father-in-law. She told me about an incident in Mexico where her father-in-law disappeared for a few days and then showed up at their hotel. He confided to her that he sometimes did undercover work for the government or rich clients. She was told to say nothing. With his disappearance for such a long period of time, she believes he is in trouble. He told her there was a job in South America, Peru specifically. Our government won't or can't help him or the daughter. There's more."

"Let's hear what else you have."

"The daughter has been trying every evening to contact her father-in-law. They had a set pattern of what time she would call. The recent call to him answered. Rather, someone hit the receive button. There was no person there on the other end. The sound was dogs barking and then the phone went dead."

Derek paced the floor and rubbed his fingers through his hair.

"Hmm, not good. I hate crossing lines with our government. We usually do the opposite and help them. Dogs could be a problem. We don't know what type of dogs, but I could guess. We have Mrs. Crandall missing and a father-in-law. They both went to South America. Let me call some people that I know. Harry Jenkins from Williamsburg, Virginia, is now with the FBI as an investigator."

"Congratulations to Harry. That's excellent news. He was on the boat with your catamaran flotilla intervention."

"That's a very nice way to call out our misfortune and screw-up with Snake woman. Harry had other successful missions which helped to transfer him into the Bureau."

"Do you think he can help?"

"It might be easier for me to get a few answers and then you can get back to the daughter. I'll need her name. Oh, see if we can get access to her cell phone calls to hear the dogs."

"Her actress name is Angela Crandall Roth. Her father-in-law paid for her career, hence the last name. Her father-in-law is Connor Roth. I'll get cracking on the cell phone."

"We're talking the actress? Now, there's lots of money. I've heard rumors about her millions."

Tami read the movie magazines and saw the number of movies the woman completed. "There's one more problem."

"What is the additional issue?"

"Mrs. Crandall's son has been following her when she is out shopping or getting a latte. He bumps into her and acts like their meeting was an accident. He always asks Angela out for a date. She has told him no repeatedly. She is about ready to get a restraining order against him. She told me that she's always been afraid of him."

"Did you make any recommendations?"

"No, I hoped that you and Brandon could talk to him first."

A week later, the two investigators visited Mrs. Crandall's son, Levan. There was a party at the house and several women answered the door. They talked with Levan who had no idea of any of his mother's plans in Peru. They went to her desk and found the travel brochure and company she used to make her reservations. She was supposed to go on a tour. They thanked Levan for the information.

Before the two men left the house, Derek informed Levan of their highly-suggested plan for his future safety. He must stay away from their new client, Angela Crandall Roth, or else. Stalking was a serious charge that could ruin his reputation with the ladies. Levan was surprised Angela hired them and accused him. He couldn't control his anger and pounded on his mother's staircase. Derek stepped toward Levan who stopped his rant. Calming down, Levan told them he didn't need to see Angela anymore because he found new friends.

Derek and Brandon were doubtful about such a quick change in his personality, but they left the premises. The men made their point.

They would find the travel agency who had other clients who disappeared. This was why the FBI was investigating. Derek offered their company's services to them to also help resolve the missing person's case for their client.

Tami and Cortez would interview the other family's whose members disappeared. Later they would travel to Peru to investigate the hotel and rental car agency. Cortez's brother would tag along.

There was safety in numbers and the brothers were excited. They felt Peru was like Miami, only more laid back. Cortez wondered if he could sneak his hamster through security. Tami told him that it wasn't a good idea. The cockroaches were too big for a hamster to eat. She told him it was the special brandy the locals made. Cortez knew his wife was teasing him.

46   Case Overload

RHONDA DROVE HER black sports car with red interior to the Los Angeles harbor. She purchased the new vehicle with the bonus she received for her promotion. The leather felt smooth and inviting. The car made her happy. However, she did have an issue with Derek.

Derek was sitting in the outside lounge of the Wright's yacht eating mixed nuts. He saw her drive into their private parking spaces and get out of the new car.

"Hello, Rhonda, it's good to see you again. Skid talked to me about your new sports car. You look great driving the wonder machine."

She handed him a copy of his note to her.

"When were you going to tell me about Seattle? Your note is a bit late about undercover activities. I know that word is in our contract, but we're friends."

Derek frowned and went to the lounge bar. He pulled out a bottle of water for Rhonda and brought the jar of mixed nuts over to her. Jess was off shopping at the mall.

"I talked with Jim when I visited the nursing home. He told me that I should talk with Simms about Seattle. Therefore, I did hear the fishing boat story at Gig Harbor. Simms helped work with the restaurant to get some photos off their security camera. I ran the photos through our face recognition program, and Snake woman was there."

"The men didn't report the incidence until a month later. I don't understand why?"

"The restaurant and party were full of patrons which could have been hurt and a potential hostage situation develop. She already calculated an escape route. Her escape could have been anything from a helicopter to riding some logging truck out of the area. The location in Puget Sound is a huge waterway of inlets, bays, and islands. That doesn't count the boats or ferries. There's the rain, the moss, the mountains, etc. The risk was too great. Then Jim had his stroke which delayed his telling us."

Rhonda opened the jar of mixed nuts and ate the two largest pieces.

"Okay, I get the picture. I've been in the area. Huge trees everywhere and logging trucks, not to mention Mt. Rainier. These nuts are addictive."

Derek grinned. He helped Rhonda calm down and she would be more receptive to his side.

"I worked the scene and kept Tiare out of the case. I did so on purpose. We don't want her involved. I promised Jess. There's also her husband, Mic, who would have tracked me down. He's very protective of her."

It was Rhonda's turn to smile.

"Just like some other husband that we know."

Rhonda dug into her briefcase. "This report came in from Mali. I wanted to bring it right over."

Derek read the lengthy report and stepped outside the lounge onto the bridge. Rhonda followed him and looked across the harbor. The pelicans were across the way on a huge rock staring into the water. Seagulls flew above. She recognized the fact that a school of fish were rippling on the water.

"What did you think of the new situation?"

"This is something highly unusual. The connection is there. We can see the association. Mali is not aware of the Los Angeles dead politician, Rich Madden. Theresa Tracker and her boyfriend, Henri Clan, more than likely killed him as well as Matin Domingo. We believe she did so without her boss, Snake woman's approval. Rich was found dead inside his vault in his house. He died from a toxic overdose of poison. The Madden family are a powerful lawyer firm in Miami. Rich had two brothers, Barry and Gerard. They vowed to hunt down and get Rich's murderer."

Rhonda shifted back from the pelican scene.

"They have connected Theresa Tracker to our Snake woman, Danielle Ashley. The Miami brothers must have read the article about her in either the African paper or the Paris paper. The Madden brothers went to Mali to find Danielle. We can assume they met Mr. Hatcher at his mine, and we see the fallout that meeting must have invoked."

"So, you believe Mr. Hatcher found out about Lachlan and his plans with Danielle?"

"Yes, I think Mr. Hatcher gave up Lachlan Thomas's name to them and the brothers plotted to capture him. Lachlan Thomas probably knows Danielle's whereabouts. Mr. Hatcher wins the prize in taking out a competitor and finding Danielle's location if the brothers are successful in their venture."

Derek asked Rhonda if she wanted some lunch.

"Maybe next time. I've got a date with Skid in an hour."

"Good. You will let the Mali police have a copy of some of our files?"

"I will do that after my lunch date."

"Fine with me."

The transformation on Rhonda's face was amazing when she talked about Skid. Derek recognized the love between his two, very favorite people. She pointed back to their report.

The report showed that Mr. Thomas sold his condominium in Hong Kong and his house in Mali to the new owners of the mine. The furniture was sold to a company who recently picked the items up and took them to their warehouse.

"He sold the mine and his house fairly fast."

"Yes, except there is more to that story."

Derek read the second section of the report. The security detail was let go and Mr. Thomas hired a limousine from the airport to take him there. On the way to the airport, Mr. Thomas stopped, went on a late ferry ride, and returned to shore. No one remembered the men on the ferry. The last ferry is always crowded. The limousine was found alongside the road on the outskirts of town minus Mr. Thomas and the driver. Mr. Thomas's luggage was still inside the car. There were traces of blood inside the passenger side and driver's side of the limousine. The police assumed that something bad may have happened to the driver and his passenger. The ocean was also searched. The Mali police interviewed another limousine driver because of their relationship to each other.

Derek read the names of the drivers. They were Barry and Gerard Madden.

"The Madden brothers went to Mali to eventually kill Danielle. They ran into Lachlan and the scene backfired."

"It appears that's true. When questioned, the two men decided to vacation in Mali for some time and thought this was a good way to meet new clients."

"The police accepted their answer?"

Rhonda said, "Their excuse sounds flimsy."

The missing driver was Barry Madden. The police noted that Gerard Madden wore facial cuts and bruises. His hands also were cut. The man explained that he fell into one of the many gold holes in the area.

"More flimsy excuses?"

"Gerard was distraught about the disappearance of his brother. Their journey to Africa was a supreme bust and failure. The disappearance was a strange case the Mali police felt was unsolvable. They regretted the loss of one of their prominent people, Lachlan Thomas and, of course, the lawyer from Miami, Barry Madden. They have closed the case due to the other cases in their files. The word used was overload."

Derek closed the folder shut and Rhonda left for her lunch date.

"Where are you Lachlan? I bet you moved all your money offshore. You knew trouble was coming. You more than likely didn't reveal Danielle's location because you were in love with her. I wonder what she will do about your disappearance. Did she arrange an exit plan, and are you with her? Dean Crain would probably take this bet. The odds are in her favor and yours regarding survival."

His lunch arrived, and Derek thanked his crew member. He dived into the roast beef sandwich crunching the lettuce. The dill pickle he saved for last and put mustard on it. Derek agreed with Simms about mustard, much to their friend, Jim's consternation. He threw the bread crust overboard for the ducks. The ducks were smart and waited for the bread. They moved fast to get out of the way of the one hundred sixty-foot yacht when the engines started. A little mustard was on the crusts.

"Smart ducks. Smart criminals."

He put the report in his scanner and sent himself the file. Next, he placed the report in an envelope with a note to his secretary. The courier would be contacted to return the report back to his office.

Derek waited for Jess to return to the yacht, so they could cruise to Catalina Island. He knew she would want to have the new information. Her thoughts about the development would be valuable. They had been working for years with the con artist and criminals. Both wanted them parked in jail or dumped permanently somewhere else.

"Annie Oakley, so much for our retirement. It looks the silver guns with pearl handles are required. My consulting is going to be more hours than we bargained for. I wonder if you will be pleased or not."

The report contained information. The information was their special word to each other. The contents were *something*.

47   Catalina Island

IN CALIFORNIA, THE quantity of average sun days near Los Angeles was many. The number of days was one hundred and fifty or more depending where a person stood. One of the perfect spots to visit on a nice day was Catalina Island. The Wrights liked to hike and bike around the area.

The Wrights anchored in Catalina Island's bay for three days. It was enough time for Derek and Jess to squeeze in a little holiday. Their twin girls were having fun with the water slide. Every time they went down the slide, one of their security divers would pop up and spray them with water. Girls their age squealed or screamed a lot. For the Wrights, the sound was a familiar one. The safety nets were out around their landing to keep creatures of the deep away. The divers in the water were extra security.

"Don't worry, Derek, they will grow up and be silent."

"You know, I think that's what I'm afraid of. At least we know where they are and what they are doing. Not to mention, with whom."

"They'll do fine in the dating world. The boys will be afraid of you. They won't do anything wrong."

Derek growled like Dean used to do.

His growl made Jess laugh.

"I remember the con artist game in San Francisco catching the tribe of thieves."

"Yes, the catch of those thieves was a walk in the park."

Derek looked at his wife in her white bikini sitting in a lounge chair. She sprayed more suntan lotion on and handed the bottle to Derek.

"I hate these bottles. In the good old days, we used oil. A man could spend hours slathering the stuff over a female frame."

Jess looked at Derek in his swim trunks.

"Oh, heavens. You are so gone."

"Yes, and you love the fact that I'm there."

His wife laughed some more.

"There is something that still bothers me."

"Oh, oh, you had to destroy my mood. What are you thinking? It can't be good."

"Then I won't tell you what has crossed my mind."

Derek knew he was in trouble. He went to the bar, opened some colas, and brought her a glass.

"Peace?"

Jess took the chilled liquid. The taste wetted her parched throat.

"Okay, thank you, for my nice refreshment. "This stuff is good."

"The champagne we have for later will be better. It was a hundred dollars a bottle. However, it was a gift from War Julio."

"Why did he send us a gift?"

Derek knew the champagne and their friend distracted her.

"His new warehouse and fish business here officially opened. The winery has put a fish label on this year's champagne. The winery will promote his fish business. It was his wife, Janet's idea."

"How terrific for them. I'm pleased."

The two sat in silence for some time. Derek finally remembered their earlier conversation.

"Jess, what did you want to tell me. It could be important."

Jess put her empty glass down on the side table. She looked at Derek. Her gray eyes were solemn.

"Did you check who the new owners were of Lachlan Thomas's mine? It seems strange that he had money but would walk away from a still workable project. The man devoted years to build the thing."

"We did check into the company. They are a solid company based in Seattle. The company is extremely profitable in their investment properties. They use their expertise to redevelop a mine to increase its potential."

"Once the mine is at a profitable potential, what do they do with the mine. Do they keep running the thing or resell the expanded mine?"

Derek sat in his lounge chair, drained his glass, and got up to get another one.

He stopped halfway over to Jess.

"That's it. She planned all of this. Granted, the whole thing has taken some time to bring to fruition. I can't believe how she pulled this off. We were totally thrown in other directions."

Jess nodded. "You said she planned the mine sale for Lachlan, rebought it with all the new equipment, extracted better grades of gold, and resold the mine again through the same Seattle company. We know she hid gold in her jars of cream. I wonder if the gold came from Bryce Hatcher's mine? If so, she and Lachlan are very rich. However, Hatcher could be a problem for them if they've escaped."

Derek handed Jess the bottle of cola.

"I've got to go check this out with the women at our office and the police. Sorry, honey, I need the helicopter to get back."

"All right, go do your detective stuff, Derek. We'll manage moving the yacht to the harbor. You have larger pursuits to follow."

Derek kissed his wife and went below to change. Jess was glad she waited. The thought about the mine occurred to her a month ago. It was when she realized Snake woman wouldn't hurt her or her family. The woman was a sharpshooter and rigged the guns in Virginia to maim. The bomb on the door at the Paris warehouse was only enough to blow the door. The sprinkler system in the entry way of the warehouse in Paris was re-engaged and the water hooked up. Hamm was the person who interfered.

Jess poured herself a second glass and wrapped her red beach towel around the waist. She went to the side of the boat for a better vantage point. Derek let his co-pilot have the controls. She waved to Derek as their helicopter lifted upward and away from the yacht.

Derek smiled. She still looked like Point Reyes Lighthouse.

Jess lifted her glass in a toast. The helicopter flew toward Los Angeles. Her girls came racing around the corner filled with excitement and very wet swimsuits. Derek looked back and saw his girls.

"My two magical sea nymphs have arrived. How about we ask the chef to make us his delicious cheese balls with milk."

The twins jumped up and down. They sang in unison, "Chocolate."

"Okay, I give. Let's do chocolate milk."

Jess hugged them before they raced to change out of their wet clothes.

She walked back to her bedroom to change. Her thoughts turned. She reflected that Danielle or Snake woman would miss this part in her life with her daughter gone.

"Money can't buy everything. Or could it?"

She had another idea. Jess decided to wait to tell Derek. The idea was filled with impossible possibilities.

"Two negatives make a positive. Multiply or divide? A person still gets a positive. This time she chose to divide and conquer."

Jess could hear Dean scolding her.

"Sometimes fate needs to be put on hold."

48 Closure

THE PRIVATE JET slowed in speed and gave the signal the altitude level was safe to open the back door. The crew member was ready with the two wreaths. There was no wire in them. The wreaths were handwoven to dissolve into the ocean below.

The man talked to the woman beside him.

"The time has come. We are approaching the location."

"Have them circle. I need to listen one more time."

"We can circle about four times only, and then we must turn the plane to our destination."

"I need this one time."

The woman went to the back of the airplane and played the message from her daughter on the burner phone. The date on the phone was about to expire.

The man looked toward the back of the cabin and hoped the message was still there.

The woman hit the message button.

"Mom, I'm settled on the plane. Thank you for trusting me to meet your new person. I'll see you shortly. I can hardly wait to eat the New York style slice of cheese pizza. The pizza is probably not as good as the slice we tasted in Boston. I know you remember that trip. The harbor was layered in fog. My flight attendant told me she'd bring my cheese pizza as soon as she could with extra packets of parmesan. Love you, mom."

The recording ended, and the woman walked back to the front of the private jet. She tried to speak. She handed the phone to him. He would take the phone to the back of the airplane. The phone would be disposed.

"It's all right. I'll release the flower bouquet for your daughter and then the other one for the other families."

The woman nodded.

The airplane door opened, and the wreaths fell into the water. The phone disappeared. All trace of her daughter was gone. She looked out the windows as the plane circled back on its route. Her man joined her in the next seat.

Lachlan held her hand.

"The flowers have descended and are free.

The woman responded, "Free at last."

Her companion knew the woman wouldn't be free of the image of her daughter for a long time. He would help her through loss.

A courier ordered a modest flower bouquet to be placed on another grave. There would be no card or florist name on the package.

She would miss her half-brother, David, too. The two of them were once inseparable. She hadn't lost track of him all these years. He never knew she paid his bail.

She and her brother learned the game of deception well. He was the person who took her to the orphanage in England, so she could have a chance. David was the one who stole the needle and thread to sew the name, Margaret, on her blouse. He was the one who found the suitcases at a thrift store with the stamps, Jamaica and Bermuda. Neither one had gone with their father to these locations. David didn't want to be with his father. Her mother took the boy into their home. They traveled to England with her mother to live.

Unfortunately for them, the mother early on developed symptoms of memory loss. One day, she and David came home. The landlord called the health authorities who took the ill woman away. The landlord moved their sparse furniture out and told the two youngsters to go live elsewhere. They lived on the streets for some time until David could get a job on a ship to America. The streets were too dangerous for them, especially a young girl.

Danielle knew David would never purposely divulge the correct information to the police or anyone. His gift was making up fantastic stories. All documents regarding her baptism were thrown away. There was no birth certificate. He believed the foundling home would create one for her. He was correct.

Another wildflower bouquet was sent to a nursing home in London. The card attached would be a beach scene of a child playing in the surf. Her mother would vaguely remember the child. The home would place the card with the other ones. The flowers came once a year on the woman's birthday. Danielle smiled.

Lachlan was talking to their pilot. They would be landing soon. She looked out the plane window. A new life was beginning.

Danielle hadn't told Lachlan about the raid happening soon at Bryce Hatcher's mine. The police would find in his warehouses gold that was not registered in the required log books to the Mali government. The amount of pure gold was slightly over the limit. The rest of the bright stuff was fool's gold. Snake woman sent her message. The man should be glad there wasn't a snake skin attached. They would put Hatch in jail. His lawyer wouldn't be able to get him out.

The new judge in Mali who presided over Mr. Hatcher's case was harsh. His name was Judge Daken from Dakar. The judge was semi-retired and loved his new job away from the criminals in Dakar, Senegal, and Guinea-Bissau. He was the judge that dealt with Santan Chesin and Sphinx Reeker. He knew the criminal con stories and games.

When Mr. Hatcher tried to blame a non-existent woman called snake, the judge shut him down. The judge wasn't interested in hearing about pyramids, strange women, and snakes. It was Mr. Hatcher's unlucky day to encounter Judge Daken. The judge's wife was named Dani after her original name,

Danielle. Every time Mr. Hatcher spoke of his issues with a woman by this name, the judge popped another anti-digestion tablet into his mouth. The judge kept looking at his watch because he didn't want to miss his golf lesson. Golf reduced stress.

By the end of the day, the judge saw only one snake in his courtroom. The snake or criminal who would serve time was Mr. Hatcher for robbing the government. At midnight, Hatch was transferred in shock to jail-hell which is what the inmates called the place. He made the mistake of tangling with a woman he shouldn't have. The dance game was rigged like a casino table at a pricey hotel. The spoils would go to the winner, or in this case, a pair of highly intelligent con artists.

Mr. Hatcher's mine was put on the auction block to pay his exorbitant attorney fees. A firm from Seattle purchased the mine. Danielle, Snake woman, found a temporary solution for her and Lachlan's enemy. She contacted the Seattle firm. They were interested in purchasing the mine.

She could hardly wait to get home to their new cottage in Oregon when renovations were completed. There was a long porch and large trees on the property. The home contained many upgrades and security. They would have to add a few more. Special garages would be built. A runway and large building were purchased close to the property. The house structure was normal in size for the area of homes located along the beach. She could see the pathway to the beach.

Danielle looked at her new diamond engagement ring. The ring held a large diamond with a plain band.

The husband and wife would blend well into the community of families in the small ocean town. The water was blue surf with gentle waves, a peaceful and serene place to take a break.

Lachlan came back and said, "Brita is going to meet us in Oregon?"

"She will be there. We've made the arrangements for her to stay on the property during the renovation. I've hired some convicts who knew my brother and are out of prison. They will be our security guards. They were loyal to my half-brother."

"This means we can fly to the Peru estate?"

"We can, and we will. I think you will like the place you purchased. It's very remote and beautiful. We do own horses and should be able to ride them on the estate."

"Horses? I have never ridden the creature. Maybe, there was a pony at some zoo. You'll have to teach me to ride."

"Riding is fun. A trainer has already been arranged."

"Is there anything else I should know about you, my ninja warrior?"

She gently shoved him away. "I don't think there is. But maybe there's a few things. Women always keep secrets."

Lachlan smiled at a memory.

One time she showed him how to escape from a police interview room. He watched fascinated at her demonstration. There were handcuffs on her legs and hands which she quickly removed, attached the metal restraints to the air vent ceiling, and swung onto the table. Landing in a split leg exercise, she moved from the split stance to a crouch, and backflipped to the floor. In a decisive move, she swung the interview room door off its hinges. The hinges were removed when she touched them earlier in a caress. This happened so swiftly when she previously entered the room, no one had a clue. The hinges were stuffed in her waistband.

Danielle told him older hinges were the easiest to remove. She asked Lachlan if he wanted to know how she restrained and immobilized her captors.

Lachlan shook his head. His guess was her shoe laces and karate training came into play.

He knew she was capable of anything. He wondered what the next revelation would be. Nothing surprised him. The man should have been scared off by her abilities. Lachlan was one to never scare easily.

49 Peru

THE HORSES WERE in the barn some distance from the estate house and caretaker buildings.

Danielle left the dogs with Lachlan and went to saddle the two horses for the new trainer and Lachlan to ride. She thought about their new airplane parked at the leased air field which was five miles away. The horses were fine, high-spirited Arabians purchased from their closest neighbor. The airplane was larger than their last one due to the distance they would fly to reach various locations.

She noticed a slight tremor on the earth below her feet. The horses were fidgety. They were fed earlier and should not be hungry. First, she saddled the older horse who was calmer and gentler. She completed the other saddle and reins, speaking gently to the horse, coaxing him to be cooperative. Closing the horse stall gates, she gave each one a carrot.

Danielle would go back to the house and meet the horse trainer, Connor Roth. She saw Mr. Roth's car in the driveway. Danielle checked out the man's website but didn't know he was a fake. He was hired by the Madden brother, Gerard, to investigate Mr. Lachlan Thomas.

She prepared the horses for the men who were starting the riding lesson at three in the afternoon.

There was a loud boom like a jet sound. She went to the barn office window which was now cracked. Grabbing the gun from the desk drawer, she looked outside.

The dirt around the top of the mountain where there were waterfalls from the past heavy rains suddenly gave way with another tremor.

"Earthquake."

Danielle looked in horror as a huge pile of earth came toward the estate structures. The house was only five years old. No one or the realtor told them about the prior slide in this area from an earthquake in 2007.

She crawled under the desk, put her leathered gloves over her ears, and stayed there until the rumbling sound diminished. Glass and breakage sounds were everywhere. Looking out the cracked glass window, she saw the buildings of Lachlan's estate were wiped off the hill. The dirt was still moving and slowly stopped. There was nothing but quiet. No movement appeared around where the house stood. Lachlan and the horse trainer were gone. Other areas were hit by the landslides. A busload of tourists disappeared.

The horses snorted their unhappiness and fear. She drew her attention to the inside of the barn. Her legs were shaking, and she grabbed the wall to support herself. The ground was rolling. The walls of the barn were thick cement and heavy beams. The motion stopped, and the barn held.

Immediately, she opened the wall safe, took out passports, id's, and money. They were thrown into a small black duffel bag. It was important to get off the ridgeline before another quake hit. She lifted herself onto the gentler horse and tied a rope to the other horse. Finding the pathway, she rode three miles to the closest ranch, put a packet of money in the saddle for their friend, opened the gate, and let the horses inside.

Their close neighbor would take care of the horses. He told them if they ever needed anything, he would be glad to help. His rich family controlled and owned the ranch for years. Their workers patrolled with guns to keep thieves away from their cows, horses, and crops. The man loved beautiful women and rich friends. He was glad to be neighbors, trusted them, and gave her the key code to unlock the back-field's gate.

She walked the rest of the way to the small airfield and hangar. Using the tractor device, she pulled the airplane onto the runway. Putting the tractor back, she locked the building and stepped into her airplane with the duffel bag.

Noting her direction and entering the data in the airplane's computer, she taxied down the small runway to make sure there wasn't any large debris. Circling back, she cranked the engines, the plane picked up power, hurled down the runway, and lifted into the skies. Danielle knew the coordinates and her destinations. They flew this route before. Their money was still in an account. They hadn't moved the money to Peru yet. She was thankfully still a rich woman.

During the flight she took a break and put the controls on auto-pilot. In the bathroom, she opened the medicine cabinet to get some aspirin. Her neck hurt from the massive strain. She accidentally glanced at herself in the mirror. A stranger's face stared at her. The woman's face was ashen. Her hair was in disarray. Dirt covered the white blouse and slacks. The vision blurred, and her real face appeared in the looking-glass. Bittersweet memories hit her. She remembered the last time they were on the airplane. Lachlan held her in his arms in their tiny bathroom.

She looked again and saw her lover's face in the mirror. Then the image vanished. Touching the cold hard surface of the mirror, she dropped the bottle. There was only one figure, the stranger. Reality of immense loss rolled into her thoughts. Holding her head, she was spinning out of control.

The pilot caved onto the aspirin-covered floor which reminded her of the diamonds and pearls he bought her in London. Images of the two of them together flashed across her vision like a Milky Way spray from the heavens. She tried to capture the mess which represented objects of importance. Diamonds and pearls slipped through her fingers. A piece of glass caught. Everything she was looking for in this world slipped through her hands once again. There was no master plan for love. The mirror was a piece of aluminum refracting light.

"Stupid mirror."

Her dreams were gone. Misery and grief overtook her body as her barriers broke apart. The stress was too much. Brokenness happened. Nothing mattered. Oblivion was where she wanted to go. Life and death didn't matter. She was at a crossroad.

There was no money in the world to ease her hurt. She lost her love and her child. Then she saw herself. She saw the child at two years old, hiding in a closet. The little girl couldn't remember why she was in the small space?

Consciousness was at bay. There was no movement. She was oblivious to the airplane and open cut on her hand. Grief overwhelmed her. Her life resonated pieces. The pieces were broken. No person was going to fix her life. Protection was off the table. All she saw was her reflection. There was only one person who could release her from the pain. She was the person standing on the top of the hill.

"Where was her strength? Would she fall?"

She had been here. Strange and lonely was familiar. She was the hill. The wind blew, swirling around the young woman.

The airplane flew onward. The airplane's software female voice spewed the GPS location, altitude, and monitoring of the airplane mechanicals. The tone came across to the empty cabin. The woman on the floor heard the voice. The voice was data. The data went unnoticed. Nothing was registering.

The beeping sound started. The auto-pilot alarm clicked the pilot back into the everyday realm of earth and its happenings. There was a mess of glass and aspirin and on the floor. She couldn't remember opening the bottle. If she stayed on the floor, the plane would crash. Recovery was imminent.

Her airplane engines were struggling with continuity. Brokenness in this hemisphere could happen with mechanical parts.

The clock was ticking. There wasn't much time. The beeping kept resounding in her head, *get up and try*. With effort, she stood up and grabbed a paper towel which she wrapped around her left hand. The plane hit some turbulence and descended. She stumbled past the seats to the cockpit. Looking out the window, the trees were close. A voice message warned her about the altitude.

She quickly went to the pilot seat and took over control of the airplane and her life.

"Let's not go crazy just yet."

The rainforests or huge trees were directly below her. She quickly scanned the guidance map one last time. The gas in the tank would be enough. She slowly banked the plane over the ocean, avoiding the proximity of the super tall trees. Her action stopped the free-fall of the airplane into nonexistence. The lower wing tip gloriously missed the tops by a few feet.

"Too close. I believe some gods are with me."

She and the plane were almost vanquished from the skies. She was whisper-close. Circling back, the pilot banked right and flew inland until she saw the forest clearing. The space looked familiar. She was close to the tiny airstrip. Familiarity engulfed her. This was her first target on the return map.

The landing would be low, tight, and fast. This dirt runway was designed for her. She was in her element. A thousand times she landed a plane in a dirt cornfield. This South American field was no different. A thousand times were her landings in more normal environments. Abnormal worked. Today was abnormal. She adapted. The woman prepared the airplane for its final descent.

"God, you have turned into a babbling idiot. You hate those types of women. Insecure comes to the forefront. Insecure means foreign. Foreign has left your body long ago. However, you have been talking to yourself for a whole day. Talking to yourself is the first sign of unstable. Derek Wright would be glad about your failure. His wife, Jess, saw a glimpse of your personality. There was no fooling Jess. She saw the Snake woman, you, for what you are--very human. Poor decision to reveal myself to Jess. My disguise didn't hold with her."

The engines of the airplane purred.

"Can't you see, Snake woman, you are the only one here. This is not your day to die. Abnormal lights give you the direction. Don't you see what is happening? Go, bogey down to solid earth. There's another day to dance. Unstable doesn't fit your mood right now. Girl, let's do this landing."

Adrenalin did a kick-start to her system. A hundred stallion horses were pulling and fueling her body. She radioed the tower and received the clearance to land.

The sleek, smooth-bodied plane obeyed her every skilled command. She stopped the airplane within a few feet of the ground handler who guided her into a dirt-packed bay. The plane was turned sideways for an easier pull onto the runway in the morning. The dust settled on her windshield and plane. They assured her the airplane and windshield would be hand-cleaned before takeoff.

She swept up the mess in the bathroom. Then she found some antibiotic, gauze, and tape for her hand. The cut was deeper than she thought. The need for stitches was thrown away. There were prescription pills on the airplane to monitor infection. She popped two into her mouth.

"Clean bandages fixed soldiers."

Stopping at the small airport office late in the evening, she looked at the board. They put her on the list of airplanes first out. They wanted her to be gone. It was what she and Lachlan paid for when they were here earlier. An escape plan was set in place before they would ever need one. Money bought all the conveniences. The office had WIFI. The woman made a phone call.

"Brita, I'm coming home to Oregon. There's been a change of plans."

There was no emotion as she punched the off button on the throw-away cell phone. Brita would get filled in about details later. Brita was loyal. The phone in the pilot's hands was thrown to the ground, crushed, and placed in the trash barrel. There were more phones in the airplane which were registered in her new name.

"Lachlan, you would want me to be free. No regrets, baby. The mirror has cleared and we're still standing in my dreams."

He told her if something happened, she could skip the flowers. He didn't understand. Flowers were important. They were the memory of freshness and life. The sweet smell was a slice of heaven. That's when a single tear fell. She wiped the moisture away and went back to the plane to sleep. Soft music was turned on the radio to sooth her frayed nerves. The seat was lowered, a soft blanket covered her, and the woman was flat out unconscious until morning. Exhaustion enveloped the tiny space.

Her man would understand the need for haste in leaving Peru. Once the police found Lachlan's body, they would photograph the Snake ring she gave him. The ring was Matin Domingo's ring. This ring was special with the hashtag marks. The marks were the same ones she drew on the wall at Shannen's Island. The police would know the ring and the fact Snake woman was at this exact location in Peru.

Early in the morning, she continued to fly north to the next privately-owned airfield. The morning sun crested the horizon, throwing light in an arc in every direction.

"The silent world is too beautiful."

Night brought out a person's fears. She had run away from the dark disaster. There would be no more allowance for the blues, climbing walls, or loss of control. She reminded herself.

"You aren't a child anymore."

The woman resigned herself to whatever fate awaited her. Freedom was there for the taking. Light purple clouds danced across the cad-orange and cerulean-blue horizon blending in a spectacular washed hue. There was enough distance from the insanity of dirt in Peru. Possibilities existed.

The pilot put her sunglasses on to reduce the sun's glare. She hummed a song from last night. It was a hard rock, magical love song. She pushed the button for the disc that played her favorites from the 80's and 90's.

"Baby, oh baby. Oh, yeah. Let's dance, love. Time to cruise."

The mood inside the airplane changed. The drums and electric guitars pushed the fever away. The sickness of distress was shoved into the back of the closet within the arms of old dolls and tattered teddy bears. She was back in the game with full knowledge of acceptance. The bathroom floor was forgotten.

"You are who you are. Maybe, I can improve myself in some new directions. Life changes people. Change could create happiness."

The change in outlook helped. The mood was lifting her spirits. She tipped the wings a little to sway to the music. The super clean airplane responded. The smooth white surface bounced air. Then she pushed the plane to a higher altitude and more acceleration.

"This airplane is design, love-personified."

The plane flew fast to its next destination. The pilot guided the plane to maximize any air stream of lift.

50   Beach Boardwalk

BRITA ASKED HER companion if she wanted some tea and apricot scones before she left the house to go shopping. The woman declined. She motioned with her hands a message of perhaps later.

The woman went out to their deck, grabbed the yoga mat, and unrolled the foam until it was flat. She did her morning exercises like she always did at nine o'clock in the morning.

She sighed. The days were long and the nights even longer. Looking toward the beach past the small boardwalk and fence, she was alone. No one was there. The gun in her pouch was unnecessary.

The woman waited for over two months. She kept hoping to see him. She saw the man in her dreams, walking toward her. The remote suggestion that he might be alive kept getting stronger.

"Are you close? Did you escape?"

She spoke to the wind.

"I need you."

The woman hadn't needed anyone for a long time, since her relationship with Matin Domingo. He cared for her as did this man. The woman wondered if she was going mad. She felt like it.

Her weight dropped even though she forced herself to eat. The smell of fresh-baked scones was still in the air. The seagulls were circling the beach. The salty spray filled her nostrils. The water in Oregon was a blue hue, almost matching the sky. The water was cold and caught one's breath away upon feet hitting surf. She stood up and put her tennis shoes on. It was time to take a walk in the beige warm sand. This was part of her morning ritual to stay fit. The scones could wait.

Suddenly, she heard someone calling her name. The name was her real one. No one knew her name now except one person. Recognition flashed across her brain. She knew the voice and looked again toward the beach. A man with a beard was walking toward her. He looked different but was the same. She couldn't believe the image. Rubbing her eyes, the man stopped. He hesitated.

"No, don't stop."

She ran to him. Nothing was going to stop her. Thankful relief washed over her. He was real.

"Hold me in your strong arms."

"I will forever." He swung her around once more, holding the woman he loved even closer. Relief washed over him. He had been unsure. A man should never keep an attractive woman waiting. He had been gone a might too long.

She shook her head and touched him.

"This is so amazing."

"My being here is hard to believe."

She found a person who was epic in her life. The loneliness was incredible without him. Loss of him in her life was massive; all her dreams stopped.

The suntanned man was glad his love remembered him. She waited. He hoped she would be alone today. Picking her up, he twirled her around a third time. He was laughing as she held him tight. Her eyes flashed. He was appreciating the beautiful embrace. Delighted and happy, the man wanted to be in her space and breathe her air. His woman hadn't found someone else. She was there in front of him. He was close *finally*.

However, he would need to explain. The man saw logic roll across her eyes. Emotion was pushed aside. He saw her do that thing repeatedly. It was part of her early training at age two to not feel. He saw brief glimpses of the real person. Lachlan knew who she was. Grounded, she was. He was tired from traveling but wanted to accommodate her many questions. Passion would come later. He would do the steps with her. There was no question about his patience abilities. He would make everything work. She waited for him, didn't she?

"Where and how did you make it out of the landslide?"

The man laughed some more. Her questions wouldn't end. He must quickly explain or else the day would become night.

"Your crazy copper bathtub with the separate ceramic sculpted feet were something I didn't want you to buy. The small angels on the top reminded me of babies. Your stubbornness wore me down. I'm very glad you did. Right now, I don't care how much that designer antique cost us. It was a lifesaver. You also paid people to build the bathroom for your object-de-art tub at the front of the house. The location was directly in line with the dugout pathway down to the beach. The pathway was another one of your projects for escape in another direction. You told me the pathway was important. And last, but not least, was the large window. Of course, the opening was too large, and we put a cheap wood frame window in place until the heavier window would arrive. I guess the copper tub went through the window and passageway like a bobsled in a test run for the big games. You were so right. I am at a loss to thank you. Most of the other dirt from the quake built up at the end of our road. Roth, however, went back to his car to get his riding gloves. I assume the impact of dirt caught him before he could get inside his vehicle."

"Mr. Roth didn't make it. I read about his body in the papers. He wasn't a horse trainer. He was a private tracker. I kept watching for your body in the newspaper. I prayed there wouldn't be anything."

"Your prayers sent images to me. I believed my death was imminent. There was closure on my part and my thoughts were, one life gone. Your face kept pushing me to want life. I can't explain what I went through. There were angel wings wrapped around me. I believed they made a mistake. The angel wings were there for our good dogs. I was a sideline. Then I remembered we found love. I swear that's when the tub lifted."

His wife could only stifle a laugh. The scene he described was unbelievable.

"That is sweet and very strange. The top part of the tub held cherubs. I like the angel-wing theory though. Evidently, you were more than a sideline to the angels. I've always been impressed with you, too. However, I'm glad they let you go."

"Your impressions might be correct. There was something good happening in the universe. Correction, our universe. Getting back to Roth, he was the devious one. I wondered why he kept asking about my gorgeous wife and wanted to meet you. He was so convincing as a trainer in our brief conversation. Gerard must have hired him?"

"Yes, we need to change your name. I know you don't want to. However, Gerard Madden may be a future problem if we don't."

"You've convinced me. A miracle happened because of your wisdom and designer plans. Fortunately, I heard the boom and felt the floor shake when I was in the bathroom. I've lived around hurricanes and earthquakes. I know to take immediate cover. The dogs followed me like they always do. I jumped into the tub with the dogs and we slid the copper top over us. Not knowing how long I was out, I awoke to one of the dogs barking. The dog dug a hole for us to breathe. Our other dog stayed with me because his foot was broken. I climbed out with the dog and we slid on the dirt down to the beach where our other dog, Michel, happily waited. Carrying Angelo with his broken foot, and Michel following, we limped down the beach to our rancher friend's house. Our friend bandaged up the foot on Angelo and we drove to the hangar. The airplane was gone. My assumption was that you made it out of the area. I knew you were alive. I couldn't contact you, because my cell phone was gone, and the power was out."

She hugged him further. There was only the two of them on a deserted beach.

He only came back because of what she divulged to him in Peru. She admitted to killing bad guys. The bad guys were a capital part of her business. There were times when innocent victims were caught in between the snake dance. She set up special victim funds for the relatives. The money was wired and given as a gift free for the next five years from a hidden compilation of accounts she created. The survivors never complained to the police about the unknown windfall of money. It was the only way she knew how to correct an error. The money was her atonement.

"Did you fly to Oregon?"

Lachlan heard her and took a moment. The woman he knew was complicated. Complication was her signature on everything. He had no clue how to find her if she truly wanted to disappear. He only wanted to be there, beside the woman he loved. He would need to tread lightly. She was the reason he was there. Everything mattered. He had no logic when it came to their plans. Change was the only item relevant. She chose.

"No, it was too risky. I flew private planes part of the way, hitchhiked, and finally made my entrance into Mexico. I stayed there some time, so Angelo could heal and get medicine. Then I left the dogs in quarantine. We can fly them back later. I have a friend at the car dealership who will make the arrangements. He let me stay in his garage. I couldn't find a burner phone and bought a pickup truck from him in Mexico. Using our horse ranch neighbor's passport and ID, I drove across the border. We'll need to mail our friend in Peru his documents tomorrow.

"I'll get one of the security guards to travel to Washington to mail them."

"Thank you for leaving some money in the saddle bags plus the horses. Our neighbor gave us our money back in full for the horses. My return was easier than expected because of the funds. I saw an outside phone once near Venice Beach, California, but was afraid. The question in my mind was whether you were here and were safe."

"Venice Beach, I've been there. By the way, I thought I was going mad without you."

Lachlan was glad he was on her list of most wanted. He was hung up on her as well.

"The whole episode scared me, too. I arrived yesterday in Oregon but saw the construction workers. Not wanting anyone around these parts to see me, I waited until morning. My truck is two miles down the beach at the scenic overlook. We'll have our security people drive the vehicle to the garage. I also wanted to make sure there were no police around."

"No police here, just us. The security people went with Brita to get supplies. I wanted to be alone to think. Now we can make plans together. This is wonderful. We've been handed a miracle, indeed. The police and others will think we are both missing or dead."

He didn't care about the police. They were separated too long. His woman looked good to him. Her hair was a blond silver color and her body looked fit and tanned. She wore colored contact lenses. He liked her new image.

"I can think of a better place called wonderful."

He snuck a kiss which led to more. She kissed him back and led him back into the house. They were alone in their designer-renovated bedroom.

The man looked around at the white leather headboard and elegant bedspread. The carpet was a smoky charcoal with two marine blue chairs. The wall contained built-in dressers, a fireplace, and large television. Another room was the huge closet with large mirrors and computer desks with gear. The view of the ocean from the bedroom was incredible. Trees framed the sides. He whistled and repeated his wife's real name.

"Very nice. The place is perfect. I will always love you, Mia Shannen. You are my heart."

He was not afraid of her or their future together. She smiled. Her world was now all right. Perfect was too dull a word. They were safe to live another spectacular one.

"I will always love you, too, Lachlan."

But first, I must show you the new art studio. There were newly-painted pictures of trees in every form. He looked at some of her aerial shots of the forests around Oregon that were clipped to each picture. The green color held an edginess. The descending sun threw shadows in every direction. The shadows were a gold, purple color. There was one picture he gravitated toward. The light was pure white against dark green. There were huge raindrops reflecting light. The drops looked like diamonds.

"I like your new cover. Artist in residence; this is brilliant."

"Thank you."

Tomorrow was enough time to select a new name out of the extra passports for him.

ХХХХХХ

She picked up the remote, pushed the button to reopen the white linen drapes over the patio doors. Lachlan was in the shower already. She slid off the silk sheets throwing the soft coverlet aside. There was only this moment in time. She quickly dressed.

"*I'm lucky.*"

She won Lachlan's love and there would be room for more joy. There was no need to run away; he cared. Mia would be safe in his arms. She could be a real and an ideal person.

She could hardly wait until tomorrow when he saw the new white sports car she purchased for him sitting in their hangar. At the time, Mia knew it was silly. The car was her substitute for flowers. So, it cost a little more than seventeen dollars and fifty cents. Multiply the number by ten thousand was more like it.

Mia got a good deal on the car. She checked into the dealership's financials. They needed to sell the vehicle or go out of business.

The business woman almost walked away from the deal. In a final plea, the salesman told her the paint color was called lit-diamond-pearl. The woman visitor at the dealership commanded the car be placed in the sunlight which was a rare day in the northwest corridor.   As they rolled the beautiful, max-to-the-max car in the sunlight, the paint job gleamed. The color matched the illusion on the airplane floor. She touched the car and the metal felt warm. She smelled the inside of the car and there was an older man's fragrance.

"Leather and spice."

The smell evoked memories of Lachlan. The car screamed, "No doubt, baby! You've got this one. True love."

There was no question about who was purchasing the super car.

"Perfect."

Mia Shannen knew no psychologist or police profiler would ever figure her out. She always planned on it.

Coming back to reality, she heard her cell phone buzz. She saw the message was from Brita. If Brita sent a text, the message must be important. She read the text.

"I saw Gerard Madden in the hardware store. He didn't see me."

Mia shook her head. She knew the Miami man would be a problem. She hadn't expected his arrival in the area so soon. Mia texted back.

"Have our security tail him. Lachlan and I will pick you up when he has moved away from the store."

Lachlan exited the shower wearing a towel and saw her worried look. She threw him his pants and shirt.

"We have a change of plans. The party's not over. Are you ready?" said Mia.

**More Exciting Books
in A Wright Series
by Author**

Linda McKown

Diamonds Blondes and Poison – Book 1

Dead On Coordinates – Book 2

Wild Golden Obsession – Book 3

No Easy Target – Book 4

Powerhouse Race – Book 5